Praise for
The Empress of Salt and Fortune

"Dangerous, subtle, unexpected and familiar, angry and ferocious and hopeful . . . *The Empress of Salt and Fortune* is a remarkable accomplishment of storytelling."

—**NPR**

"A stunning feminist fantasy . . . The subtlety and nuance of Vo's evocative storytelling lend the novella an epic, timeless feel. Equal parts love and rage, this masterfully told story is sure to impress."

—*Publishers Weekly* (**starred review**)

"Vo's debut has it all: from sapphic love to cruel betrayals; from political intrigue to lakes that glow red to ghosts that continue to walk old paths. . . . *The Empress of Salt and Fortune* will appeal to all fans of epic fantasy."

—*Booklist* (**starred review**)

"A quiet, wrenching tale of resistance, resilience, and court intrigue."

—**R. F. Kuang**

ALSO BY NGHI VO

The Empress of Salt and Fortune

WHEN THE TIGER CAME DOWN THE MOUNTAIN

NGHI VO

A TOM DOHERTY ASSOCIATES BOOK

NEW YORK

WHEN THE TIGER CAME DOWN THE MOUNTAIN

Copyright © 2020 by Nghi Vo

Cover art by Alyssa Winans
Cover design by Christine Foltzer

Edited by Ruoxi Chen

A Tordotcom Book
Published by Tom Doherty Associates
120 Broadway
New York, NY 10271

www.tor.com

Tor® is a registered trademark of
Macmillan Publishing Group, LLC.

ISBN 978-1-250-78616-6 (ebook)
ISBN 978-1-250-78613-5 (trade paperback)

First Edition: December 2020

For Meredy Marie Shipp

When the Tiger Came Down the Mountain

Chapter One

THE TAVERN WAS LITTLE more than a waxed canvas tent, tilted towards the south by the wind that rushed headlong down the mountain. The woman who tended the makeshift bar had a thin wispy mustache styled into pointed wings over her lip, and Chih took down her family history while the mammoth scouts argued outside.

"By any chance are you related to the Dong family in Baolin?" asked Chih. "They sent some children west during the famine years, and they have the same story about Lord Kang's chase that you told me."

The woman, Dong Trinh, frowned, shook her head, and then shrugged.

"Maybe," she said. "That'd be my dad's side of the family, though, and they were mostly eaten up by a walking dog curse."

"Wait, what's a—"

Before Chih could ask or Trinh could answer, the tent flap flicked open and the two scouts came back in. The elder, Ha-jun, was tall and lean for a northerner, with permanent scowl lines chiseled into his face. The younger,

Si-yu, was shorter, nearly rectangular in build. Her face was as smooth as a beach pebble and her small black eyes were as bright as polished brass mirrors. They both wore the long sheepskin coats, fur boots, and baggy silk-lined leather trousers that were practically a uniform in this part of the world, and the only thing that set them apart from the locals were the coils of braided russet hair sewn to the shoulders of their coats.

"All right," said the elder scout. "Against my better judgment, and because unlike most southerners you have the wit to be properly dressed, I have decided to allow my niece to take you up the pass."

"The offer of datura seeds didn't hurt at all," said Si-yu cheerfully, and Chih diplomatically handed over the paper packet stuffed with small black seeds. They were as common as hashish in the south, but much rarer above the snowline.

Ha-jun took the seeds from them, sliding them into his coat before nodding to Si-yu.

"All right. There and back by tomorrow, and no messing around at the way station, either, understand? We need to be back on the circuit sooner rather than later, especially if there's a real storm on the way."

Si-yu made a face at her uncle's retreating back before picking up her lance and turning to Chih.

"Well, cleric, are you ready to go?"

At the moment, Chih didn't look much like a cleric. Their indigo robes were rolled up tightly at the bottom of their single bag. Under their fleece-lined hood, their usually shaved scalp was covered with a bristly inch of dark hair. Singing Hills was far less strict about robes and deprivations than other orders, but Chih would need a barber before they made it home.

"All set. Are we leaving soon?"

"Right now, if you're ready. We can make the way station by dark with just a little bit of luck."

Chih followed Si-yu into the dry and scouring cold, shuddering a little in spite of themself. The wind bit into their bones and left them oddly sore and sleepy, and they shrugged a little deeper into their coat.

"Aren't you meant to have a little recorder bird with you?" asked Si-yu, leading them down the single street of the rickety little town. There were similar towns scattered all along the border, hardscrabble little places that mushroomed when gold was discovered five years ago. The gold vein had played itself out in three years, and now there was something haunted about the whole region.

"Yes, my neixin, Almost Brilliant," Chih said with a sigh. "She's sitting a clutch of eggs right now, and this cold would be too much for her anyway."

Silently, they offered a quick prayer up to Thousand Hands for Almost Brilliant's comfort and safety. They had sorely missed the neixin's supernaturally good memory on their current trip, but it was more than that. It felt downright unnatural to be out in the world without Almost Brilliant's sharp words and good advice.

"Hopefully, when her children are grown, she'll want to come out with me again. We've been together since I first got my marching orders."

"May the Master of the Sky will it so," said Si-yu. "I've always wanted to meet a neixin."

They came to a fenced paddock, a rudimentary wood structure that looked as if it did not have the strength to hold back much more than a small flock of disinterested rocks. Beyond narrow rails were—

Chih had seen them from a distance before, and given the northern countries' long and storied history, there was not much need to document them for Singing Hills, though of course Chih would do so anyway.

The mammoths in the frozen paddock were the lesser breed, smaller, slender-legged and with shorter trunks than their royal cousins. This lot mostly belonged to a breeder who was bringing them east to one of the outposts there, and they were largely russet-hued, some with a white foot or a splash of white on the topknot of fur sitting over their brow.

It seemed to Chih that they regarded the fence with a friendly condescension. If she wished to do so, the smallest among them could knock the rails aside. Instead, they chose to display their good manners by refraining and dozing on their feet, occasionally sweeping fodder into their mouths from the sheltered troughs.

It was the royal mammoths, almost half again as big and colored a deep and rusty red, that had beaten back the soldiers of the Anh empire more than fifty years ago, but the lesser mammoths had done the rest, charging through the snowy battlefields with their small ears standing straight out from their heads and bugling furiously.

"Don't be impressed with *those*," Si-yu said scornfully. "Save it for Piluk."

She whistled twice and a mammoth a touch smaller than the rest officiously pushed her way through the small herd and walked over to where Si-yu waited with open arms. Piluk, Chih saw, was darker than the others, no spot of white on her, and her long fur shaded towards black at the tips.

"This is my baby. She's from a sister line of the great Ho-shuh," Si-yu said, and Piluk's mobile trunk came down heavy and companionable around her shoulders as if in agreement.

"You can tell me exactly what that means on the road," Chih said with a grin. "She's a beauty."

"Tsk, don't compliment her in front of the others.

They'll get jealous, and then they'll refuse to do anything until you praise them as well. You can only praise a mammoth when you are alone with her and no one else can hear."

"I am going to put that into my record, and when I get home, it will be copied twice over into the volumes kept at Singing Hills. You must be very careful about what you say to me, or you may go down in history as a liar," said Chih in amusement.

"Who's lying? Come on. I'll show you how to mount a mammoth, and then you'll have to paint me in a better light."

Si-yu scaled Piluk's side so fast that Chih thought at first she must have simply grabbed great handfuls of Piluk's long fur to help herself up. When they looked more closely, however, they could see that there were loops of leather hanging down from the saddle close behind Piluk's neck, one longer and one shorter.

"Hand in the shorter, foot in the longer, that's right, just like that, and then wait for the push."

"Wait, the push . . . ?"

Piluk's foot kicked back, gentle for such a large animal, and Chih yelped as they were suddenly pushed up bodily. They would have planted face-first in Piluk's dense fur, but Si-yu reached over to grab Chih's shoulders and to drag them the rest of the way up.

"How strong *are* you?" asked Chih in surprise, and Si-yu laughed.

"Strong! I'd flex but it's not like you could see through my coat, anyway. Here, sit like I am . . ."

There was a horn carved from bone sticking up out of the head of the saddle around which Si-yu had curled her knee, the other leg hanging down opposite. There was a second shorter horn behind her, and clumsily Chih copied Si-yu's pose.

"Other way, we don't want to make her list."

The broad saddle straddled Piluk's shoulders, set back from her surprisingly narrow neck. There was no way to sit astride, so the northern cavalry all rode side-saddle. Chih adjusted their seat, and Si-yu used her long steel-tipped lance to urge Piluk towards the edge of town.

As they moved among the shacks, Chih was startled by how very far they were above them. They weren't as high up as they would have been on a royal mammoth, but the tops of the sheds barely came up to their knees, and Chih felt a giddy sense of vertigo at the base of their belly.

"If you're going to be sick, do it over the side," Si-yu said without looking back. "Otherwise you're brushing Piluk down tonight."

"I'm not going to be sick, and show me how to brush her anyway," Chih retorted. "I'll be fine."

As they left the town and started climbing the road towards the pass, Chih could already feel the burn in their thighs and their lower back. Si-yu sat as easily as if she were on a cushion at home, but Chih's muscles were better used to long walks, and, if they were entirely honest with themselves, hitching rides in the back of oxcarts.

Well, at least Almost Brilliant isn't here to make fun of me.

The road through Kihir Pass was steep and wide, bordered on both sides by thick boreal forests. It was home to ghosts, which bothered Chih very little, and bandits, which were more of an issue. Chih had interviewed plenty of bandits over the course of their career, but times had been a little lean lately, and they hadn't felt like taking the risk. Neither ghosts nor bandits would bother two people on a mammoth, however, and anyway, Chih had never been on a mammoth before. What was the point of being a Singing Hills cleric if they didn't get to ride a mammoth when the opportunity arose?

The novelty wore off, but the wonder didn't, and Chih ignored the growing aches in their knee and lower back as they looked down on the world around them, listened to the jangling of Piluk's iron bells, and hunched behind Si-yu as they pressed into the wind.

Around noon, or what Chih guessed to be noon given the thin gray light, Si-yu brought Piluk to a halt in the shelter of a dense copse of trash pine. Chih was relieved to be returning to level ground, but then they watched in dismay as Si-yu seemed to simply slide straight down the mammoth's side, landing with a little *pah* of exertion.

"Do I have to do that?" Chih called, and Si-yu grinned.

"You do if you want to eat and piss."

Chih did, and taking a deep breath, they threw their legs over and pushed themself off the side, sliding down Piluk's shoulder. They hit the ground with their knees bent, but still pitched forward right into Si-yu's waiting arms.

"There you go, well done!" said Si-yu brightly, and Chih groaned.

"You can speak to me as if I were a child all you like, just don't let go."

Obediently, Si-yu wrestled Chih over to a sheltered spot behind the trees. Fortunately, Chih's legs steadied enough so they could handle their ablutions themselves, and then they returned to where Si-yu stretched out on a waxed tarp, legs spread in a nearly perfect split.

"Should I be doing that too?"

"It'll help."

Chih managed to get onto the ground without dropping, stings of pain going through the knee that had been bent around the saddle horn and lancing through their core. They weren't as limber as Si-yu, but they thought they were doing well until the scout turned almost all the way behind her and pulled her bag forward. Chih sighed, sprawling limply on the tarp, and took the small parchment packet that Si-yu handed to them.

"How long did it take to get that flexible?" they asked, nibbling at the dried slivers of pounded reindeer meat inside.

"I just stayed good from when I was a kid. My family's been in the corps since Mei-an's day."

"That was back during the Xun Dynasty, wasn't it?"

Si-yu shrugged.

"We don't really count back from the Anh kings," she said loftily. "That's some two hundred years ago."

They of course *had* counted by the Anh system until just sixty years ago, when the southern defenses failed and the northern mammoths stormed the mountain passes. Anh had forced the north into their reckoning, and just a short while later, the north had forgotten every bit of it.

Chih did not say anything about that. Instead, they tilted their head curiously.

"That's a long time to be in the corps, isn't it?"

"Very," Si-yu said with pleasure.

"And no interest in being . . . I don't know, palace officials or judges or scholars?"

Si-yu snorted.

"What are you, a spy from Ingrusk? No. Why would I

when I've got Piluk and the first daughter she calves?"

The mammoth corps was famous, and for that, among other reasons, they were forbidden from taking state examinations of any sort or holding any position beyond that of a district official until there had been no member of the extended family in the corps for three generations. Assassination by mammoth had a rather storied history in the northern countries, but it wasn't the kind of history that anyone thought bore repeating.

Finally, Si-yu stood up with distressing ease, giving Chih a hand up as well. As they walked back to Piluk's side, Si-yu turned to Chih for a moment.

"Wait, aren't you meant to be a vegetarian? All the southern clerics . . ."

"Oh, Singing Hills isn't very strict on that," Chih said vaguely. "And we're meant to take the charity of others where we find it. It's significantly worse to turn down genuine charity than to momentarily put aside the strictures of your order, or so I was taught."

"Well, I do have some salted dried lichen for—"

"I like meat, and I am far away from anyone who might stop me," Chih said bluntly, and Si-yu grinned.

"I will keep that in mind."

Chih groaned when they reached for the saddle loop, but they managed to get back into the saddle with only a single snicker from Si-yu, so they decided to call it a victory.

The wind bit into the bare skin around Chih's face over the tall collar of their sheepskin coat. It was a tiring kind of cold, and by the time the sun sank beneath the tips of the pines, they were wavering in the saddle. Si-yu had suggested strapping them in, but Chih shook their head. They didn't like the idea of being strapped in, and the ground was not so far to fall if Si-yu allowed them to do so.

The wind picked up strength and malice as the sky went dark, and now it felt as if it were rushing through the very seams of their clothes. They thought briefly of the delirium produced by the cold on the steppe, the type that might drive someone to start stripping to relieve themselves of phantom burns. Out of the corners of their eyes, they started to see brief streamers of light, gleaming like sparks from a fire before they disappeared.

"Do you have fireflies up here?"

"What?"

"Little insects. They flash light as they fly about."

"No. You might have seen a babyghost, though. They glow like little fires in the trees before they float up and are eaten by the stars."

"They—"

"There! Up ahead."

The snow had mostly stopped, but for a moment,

Chih had no idea what Si-yu was speaking about. Then they saw the tilted roof of the way station as well as the faint gleam of a lantern glowing in the single oil-paper window.

As if picking up on her rider's excitement, Piluk snorted, hurrying up the road.

"Usually this is Bao-so's watch," Si-yu explained. "He's a friend of my mother's, used to ride with the corps until his knees gave out. You'll like him."

Chih was about to say that they were sure they would, but a low and thunderous growl started up on their left, and then on their right. A deep and jagged snarl erupted from behind them, like something tearing through the stretched and scraped skin between the world of the flesh and the world of the spirit. Piluk bugled with alarm as Si-yu swore.

It was as if the mammoth they rode were the world, and the world had gone stock still with fright beneath them.

Then Si-yu's lance flew down to smack solidly along Piluk's side and the mammoth lurched forward.

Chapter Two

"**HANG ON,** because I am *not* coming back for you!" Si-yu roared, and Chih hunched down behind her, wrapping their arms desperately around Si-yu's waist. Their legs cramped from clinging as hard as they could to the saddle. They suddenly regretted turning down the straps.

Whatever that is out there—

"Tiger," Si-yu chanted. "Tiger, tiger, *tiger . . .*"

More than one, Chih realized, seeing the streak of dull orange on one side and then the other.

They're not pack animals, they don't hunt together, they had time to think, and then Piluk crested the final rise to the way station.

"There's a barn, we can get ourselves in and Bao-so . . ."

Chih could see the slope of the barn's roof beyond the way station itself, but between them was a figure—no, two figures—on the ground, they realized after a moment.

On his back, face obscured by the hood of his sheepskin coat and arms thrown out as if he had hoped to catch himself, was Bao-so. A stocky naked woman bent over him, and she draped her arm over his belly with a casual ownership, immune to the blistering cold. Bao-so's hand twitched and the woman reached down, looking for all the world as if she wanted to hold it.

Chih froze in horror, but Si-yu only gave Piluk another hard whack, sending her lunging forward with a squeal. The mammoth's speed was ponderous, but it was like a mountain had started to move. If it was coming for you, you didn't care how fast it was coming, and that was apparently what the naked woman thought as well because in two bounds she was away and lost to the shadows.

Chih cried out when Si-yu vaulted off the side of the mammoth, throwing herself down to dash her brains out on the road, but then they realized that they were looking at the sole of Si-yu's boot, the rest of her dangling down over the side of the saddle. Si-yu's foot was caught in one of the leather loops hanging from the saddle, flexed to hook her into place.

The moment stretched out, and Chih's training forced them to notice that the soles of Si-yu's boots were stitched with faded sinew that had once been dyed green. Then they leaned over to see that Si-yu had grabbed up the man on the ground, hanging on as best she could while shouting a command to Piluk. The mammoth's head spun around, her trunk came lashing back, and Chih flinched as the muscular trunk connected with Si-yu. For a moment, it looked as if the blow had sent Si-yu and her burden flying, but then Chih saw that it had helped Si-yu regain her seat and drag the terribly still man with her.

"Grab him!" Si-yu yelped. "Cleric, *help* me!"

That broke Chih out of their daze. They helped drag the man, surprisingly light, more like a bundle of twigs in a sheepskin coat than a man, up across the mammoth's back. Somehow, he ended up facedown over Chih's lap. The saddle horn would have dug terribly into his belly if he had been conscious, but he wasn't, and then Si-yu was sending Piluk racing for the barn, the mammoth bellowing the whole time she went.

Piluk shivered and shook underneath them, and Chih winced when she tossed her head from side to side, trying to face the growls that filled the twilight. Their fingers ached from hanging on to the man Si-yu had rescued, but Chih clung as best they could. They could not fall.

The barn was a hefty thing, built of notched logs and open on one side. It was big enough that Piluk could fit into it with room to spare, and tall enough that they and Si-yu could fit under the roof with only a slight duck. By the time they reached it, Piluk was moving at a dead run, ears flared out to either side and squalling furiously.

For just a moment, Chih caught a glimpse of gleaming round eyes in the dark, and then they saw the tiger dash out of the barn, as low to the ground as a python, neatly avoiding Piluk's broad feet.

"They won't rush Piluk or any mammoth head-on," said Si-yu. "They wouldn't dare. We'd be as safe as keppi eggs if we had another two scouts with us. Even Uncle and his Nayhi, that'd be enough, they would never."

A quick command got Piluk turned around with remarkable speed and dexterity, whirling about so quickly that her iron bells jingled and her long fur swung. Chih, a little taller than Si-yu, didn't duck a rafter fast enough. There was a sickening rash of pain at their temple, and then it was only cold and wetness and a light-headed determination to hang on as tight as they could.

A moment later, everything was still, and the world in front of the barn was empty, silent. A nuthatch's soft whooping call gave the twilight a strangely normal feeling, and Chih swallowed back their panic with a gulp.

Of course it's normal. Tigers have dinner every night they can, don't they?

Si-yu waited for a moment, and when no tigers appeared to menace them, she nodded. She leaned forward, far enough that Chih thought she might fall despite everything, and she grasped Piluk's ear, whispering something into it.

Chih's fingers tightened reflexively into Bao-so's coat as the world seemed to rock underneath them, but it was only Piluk settling down, first on her hindquarters and then with her forelegs stretched in front of her, knees bent so that her round feet were flat on the ground.

Si-yu slid down to the ground, and Chih, as carefully as they could, lowered the unconscious man across their lap after her. Chih was shaking so much that it took them several deep breaths to finally unwind their leg from the saddle horn and to make their way to the ground. They let out a sigh of relief when they were free of the saddle, but then there was a flash of orange out of the corner of their eye, there and gone again in the foliage beyond the barn. In another half hour, probably far less, it would be full dark, and they wouldn't even see that.

"They're still there," Chih hissed, shrinking back against Piluk's hairy side even as Piluk shifted restlessly.

"It's fine for now. Well, not fine, but they won't rush us while Piluk is facing the entrance."

Si-yu was calm enough that Chih decided to be calm as well, and they came to kneel opposite Si-yu on the other side of the older man's body.

Even by the fading light, his skin was parchment-pale and the corners of his mouth were drawn painfully tight. For a moment, they were certain that Si-yu had done that daring bit of riding for a corpse, but then they saw the slight rise and fall of his chest. It was ragged, and there was a stutter to it that made Chih nervous, but it was still there.

"Thank the Sky, oh thank the Sky," Si-yu murmured, clasping her hands in front of her mouth. Her hood fell back, and she looked young then, too young by far.

"What's wrong with him?" Chih asked, their voice hushed.

"More like what's not wrong with him," Si-yu said. "His skull isn't cracked. His stomach hasn't been chewed open."

Si-yu took a long wavering breath and sat up straight, pulling Bao-so's hood more securely around his head.

"He's breathing. As long as he is breathing, we can say that he will be fine."

Chih smiled a little.

"That was some riding you did."

"If only riding were enough."

"What do you—"

Si-yu nodded towards the open front of the barn, and when Chih turned their head to look, their breath snagged hard in their throat, threatening to choke them.

Three tigers waited beyond the shelter of the barn, and as the last of the light faded from the sky, the largest one started to laugh.

Chapter Three

CHIH REMEMBERED A STORY that said it was tremendously unlucky to hear a tiger laugh, but they couldn't remember why. Was it a cultural taboo? Was it a curse? Was it simply that tigers thought that killing and eating people was funny? They wished they could remember. They wished they could stop shaking. They wished the tigers would simply leave.

None of those things happened, and Piluk lumbered back to her feet, snorting and tossing her head from side to side. Si-yu rose to stand next to the mammoth with her lance gripped tight in her hand, but Chih could see that the scout was shaking.

"They won't come to meet Piluk head on," she repeated. "They're cowards, they won't come close if she's facing them . . ."

"You may stop saying that at any time," said the largest tiger, and there was something so inhuman about it, words shaped in a tiger's throat, that Piluk pawed at the ground, bugling in alarm, and Si-yu had to pull Chih back before Piluk's trunk knocked them off their feet.

"Stop it!" Si-yu cried. "Stop it, talk like a person!"

No, no, the tiger is *a person. It is only that the tiger is a person that might eat us if we get too close,* Chih thought, but before they could shape that thought with their mouth, the tiger made a chuffing sound, still threatening, less unnatural.

For a moment, the air between the barn and the tiger grew strangely dense, thick like boiled gelatin or a soupy fog, and then instead of a tiger, there was a woman there, the same one that Chih had seen momentarily next to Bao-so's prone body.

The woman was of medium height, and her thick black hair was braided and coiled into multiple loops secured to her head by a wooden comb. Otherwise, she was completely naked, her body thick and strong with small breasts set high on her chest, and a belly halved with a heavy crease that sagged just a little towards her thick powerful thighs. She was a handsome woman, but the animal impassivity of her eyes and the way her teeth looked a little too large for her mouth gave her a menacing look, the tiger in her sitting in wait beneath her human skin.

"There," she said. "Now bring out the man so that my sisters and I might eat him."

Si-yu growled, and Chih swallowed hard before speaking up. It was a small chance, but then, so was their chance of getting through this without something going terribly wrong.

"Begging your pardon, Your Majesty, but our laws do not allow this," they tried.

"Your Highness?" echoed Si-yu, but Chih could see the tigers' ears flatten momentarily in understanding.

The naked woman, her face inexpressive and unable to gesture with her whiskers or her ears, nodded and sighed.

"Ah. You are something like a civilized thing, and I suppose that I must treat you as such."

"We would much prefer it, madam," Chih said respectfully, and the tiger turned towards the darkness, though her two sisters stayed to watch like guardian lions.

"Did you send them away?" Si-yu whispered urgently, and Chih shook their head.

"No. How long before your uncle comes looking for you?"

"Late afternoon tomorrow," Si-yu said, biting her lip. "Maybe tomorrow night. If the storm comes early . . . not until it's over."

"All right. Then we're going to hope he's coming by tomorrow afternoon. The tiger who is speaking, call her *Your Majesty* when you first speak to her, and then *madam* after that. Her sisters are ladies. Do *not* confuse them . . ."

"Why are we talking to tigers?" asked Si-yu.

"Because they are talking to us," Chih said, stifling a somewhat hysterical giggle. "They can talk, and now they've seen that we can. That's—that means that they'll treat us like people."

"But there's still a chance that they're going to eat us."

"Oh yes. Some people are just more . . . edible than others if you are a tiger."

Si-yu stared, but then the woman came back. The firelight glittered over the garnet threads woven through her stiff black tunic. It had a high collar like the robes worn in Anh, but it came down nearly to the jeweled slippers on her feet and was split up to her waist on both sides over wide white silk trousers. Rough rubies dangled from her ears, and she had painted her lips with red cream. She looked beautiful, and dressed for summer while the wind left ice crystals in her hair, she was certainly no human.

But a person and a queen, and if we can remember that, we might be all right.

The tiger settled on the ground at the mouth of the barn, as at home as a queen would be in her palace. After a moment, her two sisters came to lie down on either side of her, and she stretched out between them, her feet pressed into one's belly while looping her arm around the other's neck.

"I am Ho Sinh Loan, and here is my sister Sinh Hoa and my sister Sinh Cam. I am the queen of the Boarbacks and the march to the Green Mountain. Tell me your names."

Si-yu's people didn't call the mountains they stood on the Boarbacks, but it certainly wasn't the first time that Chih had dealt with alternative geography. By Chih's best guess, the tiger had just claimed the entire mountain chain and most of territory known in the north as Ogai as well. The Ogaiese would be startled to find themselves under the rule of a tiger, but it wasn't as if she were levying taxes or soldiers.

"Your Majesty, I'm Si-yu, daughter of Ha-lan and descended from the Crane from Isai. This is Piluk, by Kiean out of Lotuk."

The tiger nodded and turned to Chih expectantly.

"Madam, I'm Cleric Chih from the abbey at Singing Hills. I've come—"

"To be dinner, I think," said the tiger cordially. "All three of you will be. The mammoth can go home if she wishes."

"The *mammoth*—" Si-yu started angrily, but Chih elbowed her and she shut up.

"I'm afraid our laws do not allow it," Chih repeated. "Madam, I have come north instead to listen to your stories and to glorify your name."

"Flattery, cleric," said the tiger. "It doesn't taste very good, and it has never filled a stomach."

"History, madam," Chih responded hopefully. "History and your place in it. We have the stories of Ho Dong Vinh and Ho Thi Thao, and—"

"Ho Thi Thao?"

The tiger spoke sharply, and at her side, her two sisters sat up, their eyes narrowed and their whiskers pressed aggressively forward.

"Cleric, what have you done?" asked Si-yu flatly, and Chih resisted the urge to shrink back a little from the display of predatory interest.

"What do you know about Ho Thi Thao?" asked the tiger.

"Well, my job is rather to find out what you know," Chih said, remembering at the last moment not to smile. Smiling bared teeth, and Chih knew that theirs would not hold up next to the tiger's.

"Singing Hills does archival and investigative work, and I know for sure that we would love to have your account of the marriage of Ho Thi Thao."

"Our account," sneered the tiger. "You mean the true one."

"Of course," Chih said brightly.

"No, I don't think so."

"Then . . ."

"No, I think you are going to tell us what you know instead," said Sinh Loan.

"We'll tell you when you get it wrong," growled Sinh Hoa abruptly, her voice like falling rocks. "We shall correct you."

"Best not get it wrong too often," advised Sinh Cam, her voice like dangerous water.

"What are you *doing*?" hissed Si-yu.

"Telling a story," Chih said, and they wished that Almost Brilliant was there to scold them for such a foolish thing.

~

The tigers waited patiently as Si-yu and Chih built up the fire, Sinh Cam even briefly turning into a human to drag over an armload of firewood from behind the way station. She was younger than Sinh Loan; Chih guessed that both she and Sinh Hoa were, given how they deferred to their sister. When Chih and Si-yu came forward to take the gift of wood, Chih saw that Sinh Cam's face was completely still, as if she were not used to human expression, and that she gave off an odor of mud and cold and clean fur.

As Chih built the fire, Piluk made an uneasy groaning sound, swaying from foot to foot like a nervous child. She bumped Chih with her trunk gently, as if trying to draw their attention to the three predators lounging at the mouth of the barn.

"I know, baby," Chih said. "It's all right."

"It might be," Si-yu murmured, rising from Bao-so's side. "He woke up enough to say a few words to me and to ask for water. He's not in tremendous shape, but he'll last. If we don't all get eaten."

"Oh it could be much worse," Sinh Loan said cheerfully. "His heart has grown steady now, not jumping around like Hare at the sun's feast."

Si-yu made a face, and Chih reminded themself of how good tiger ears were.

Finally there was a fire roaring between them, built well enough to last the night, if they lasted all night. When they finally sat down by the fire, they felt colder immediately, and Chih gratefully took the extra blanket that Si-yu offered.

Piluk had settled down, still uneasily whimpering from time to time, but easier now that Si-yu had dragged Bao-so close and came to sit next to her as well.

Chih looked through the flames at the three faces watching them hungrily, took a deep breath, and began.

Chapter Four

MANY YEARS AGO, there lived a scholar named Dieu, who had studied for eighteen years and whose tutor finally reckoned that she was ready for the imperial exams in Ahnfi.

In those days, Ahnfi was the greatest city in the world, from the shores of the Mother Sea to the dry places where the dragons' bastards lurked in the black sand dunes. To be anyone who was anyone, you should have been born in the capital to one of the six great families, ideally as an able-bodied eldest boy, ideally without a single mark on your skin and without a taste for esoteric magic or radical politics. Since most people in the capital could not even manage this small thing, the next best thing was to excel at the imperial examinations, held every four years in the Hall of Ferocious Jade.

Unlike the examinations at the provincial and commandery levels, which took place every other year, the imperial examinations were dazzlingly complex, dangerously competitive, and thanks to some eight generations of mysterious deaths in the Hall of Ferocious Jade, more than a little haunted. The candidates came from all over the empire, and the prestige, wealth, and power of an imperial appointment meant that no one who had come so far intended to go home with anything less than top marks.

Dieu's great-grandfather had finagled a pass to the imperial examinations and then got assassinated before he had gotten a chance to use it. Her grandmother would have gone to the examinations, but she got distracted by a life of crime in the high mountain passes. Dieu's father might have been a fine scholar, but he died young with his wives in a river fording as they fled from their enemies one terrible autumn night.

So in the end, there was only Dieu left, living in a tiny house in Hue County, being raised by a series of diligent tutors and compassionate maids. There was a hawthorn tree in the front, a tiny garden in the back, and a wind from the north that seemed to blow as much good as bad. The house was rented, so she truly possessed only few treasured books, a face that was long and oval like a grain of rice, a mouth that smiled rather too little, and a little jade chip that guaranteed the bearer entry to the imperial examinations.

She was an over-serious girl, and years of studying late into the long Hue County night left her with an inclination to slouch. Except for the slouch, she would have been tall, and except for her squint, likewise acquired, she might have been passingly pretty.

Instead, Dieu was well-read in the classics, clever with compositions and translations, and versed in the many laws of the land. At the age of twenty-eight, her tutor nodded and collected enough money to purchase for her a suit of good traveling clothes, a decent map, a few paper talismans, and a little embroidered bag on a woven string so she could wear the jade chip around her neck.

"Well, I have taught you all I could teach you," he said to her one crisp fall morning. "You are as ready as anyone can be to enter the Hall of Ferocious Jade and emerge a court official rather than a bundle of bones tied up with your own guts—"

~

"Oh!" Sinh Cam exclaimed, sitting up in surprise. "That's right! A bundle of bones tied up with their own guts, that's what we say."

"It's a tiger's term?" Chih asked. "I thought it was just what the ghosts of the examination hall did to those scholars who who didn't follow the proper sacrifices . . ."

"No, it's ours," said Sinh Loan pleasantly. "It's what we call someone who is a disappointment. Because that's what we turn them into. Please continue."

"Of course."

~

"I'm not sure I'm ready," Dieu said. "I still have to memorize the lesser chrestomathies, and I feel like I still have a ways to go on the errata of the greater ones. And my Vihnese is still—"

"I don't think they really test on the lesser chrestomathies any longer," her tutor said with confidence, "and who speaks Vihnese anymore, anyway?"

"Well, the Vihnese do . . ."

"And I have every confidence that you will excel as it was expected that your great-grandfather would have done. You come from a good family, you are tenacious, you love the intricacies of the classics and how they bind the world to lawful congress, and anyway, the money is quite gone, and so your instruction is at an end."

Dieu understood that at least, and nodded dejectedly, though she remembered to pay proper obeisance and thanks to her tutor before he set off for points unknown.

Then she handed the keys to the small house with the hawthorn tree in Hue County over to the impatient landlord, took a last long look around the town she had never left in all her life, and started the long trek east.

~

"Oh, we never knew any of that about Dieu," rumbled Sinh Cam, and Sinh Loan nodded speculatively. Their faces possessed a similar curiosity, a strange thing to see stamped on the face of both a woman and a tiger. Sinh Hoa had dropped her head to her large paws, and she only blinked sleepily at the fire.

"It is appropriate they know more about Scholar Dieu," Sinh Loan said finally, glancing down at her neatly filed nails. "Dieu was, for all of her blessings and beauty, actually a human after all. Next, you must speak of Ho Thi Thao."

Sinh Loan sat up straight, giving the impression of a cat setting her tail neatly around her toes.

"Please, continue."

Chih swallowed, remembered not to smile, and obeyed.

Chapter Five

IN THOSE DAYS, Ahn was not the great empire it would grow to be. It was instead one of sixteen warring states that had all declared themselves the heirs of the great doomed Ku Dynasty. Some had good claims, some had large armies, and it would take at least another generation or so before the true heir to the Ku emerged.

It was through this landscape of war and contested territory that Dieu traveled, and she might begin her day in land controlled by Ing, steal behind the lines of a battle between Ing and Fu-lan, and drink her evening tea on the banks of the river claimed by Vihn.

She had turned out to be a better traveler than she had thought, or at least, she had not been eaten by hungry ghosts or had her skull stolen by fox spirits yet. She had mostly stopped panting whenever she needed to climb a rise, and she had learned early on that you never passed a priestess and her road shrine without offering something, even if it was only a tiny coin, a bun, or a prayer.

Not long after Dieu skirted the Battle of Kirshan—where General Peirong was killed by a raging bull that went on to become the king of Kirshan—she came around a bend in the road to find a small shrine to the goddess Xanh-hui. Behind its iron grating, the upright cabinet contained the goddess's sigils, a rod and a stoppered pot of healing salve, but sleeping in front of the shrine was the least likely priestess that Dieu had ever seen.

The priestess was a short, squat woman who wore a sleeveless tunic even in the flurry of late spring snow, and instead of trousers and shoes, she went barefoot under a kilt made from the tanned hide of a slate-blue calf. Her hair was loose and tangled, and the only thing that identified her as a priestess at all was the necklace of rough amber beads around her neck from which hung a small wooden carving of the goddess Xanh-hui herself.

~

"Oh," exclaimed Sinh Cam. "That's Ho Thi Thao!"

"We know," Sinh Loan said patiently.

"She wore a calfskin kilt because she stole one of the sacred calves from the sun."

"We know," Sinh Loan repeated, and Chih sat up a little straighter.

"Actually, I don't know that story," they hinted.

"Well, now you do," said Sinh Cam, pleased.

Sinh Loan sighed, reaching over to ruffle her younger sister's ears.

"She did," Sinh Loan said. "When she was very young, her mother told her that she would be forced to eat scraps all her life. She said that Ho Thi Thao was so small that she would trail behind even the pine trees that cared for nothing that tasted good or ran fast."

"Oh, what a cruel thing for a mother to say," Si-yu said, and instead of being angry, Sinh Loan inclined her proud head.

"It was. And so to prove her honorable mother wrong, Thi Thao sneaked up to the manor of the sun, where she killed the two cowherds by catching them when they were asleep, and after she ate them, she killed and ate one of the sun's most precious calves. Then she went home, ate up all the pine trees in Jo Valley, all of the humans, and then her siblings and then her mother."

"Oh," said Si-yu faintly, and Sinh Loan smiled briefly at her before turning to Chih.

"There is an addition for your books, cleric. Make a note of it so that they will find it after we eat you. Please continue."

~

Dieu went to put a coin in the bowl at the priestess's feet, and the priestess came awake with a growl, grabbing her hand before she could complete her obeisance.

"What in the world are you doing?" demanded the priestess.

"I was making an offering," said Dieu, and now she noticed things she had not seen before. She could see how there were spots of dried blood on the priestess's tunic, and how her fingernails were thick and white. Priestesses smelled like forbearance and cheap incense, not raw earth and full bellies, and Dieu did her best not to pull her hand from the woman's grasp.

"Let me see what you are offering," the woman said, and she made a face when she saw the coin.

"Oh, that's not worth anything at all."

"It's . . . worth one sen or four fi?" suggested Dieu, but the woman shook her head.

"Nothing at all," she declared, and she smacked Dieu's hand so that the coin fell into the dirt and rolled away. "What are you going to give me instead?"

"Um. I could say a prayer for the sorrow and suffering of the world . . ."

"No, I don't want that. What else do you have?"

The woman still smelled full, but there was something in her voice that suggested that was a temporary state, and her eyes, which were round and very lovely, took on a kind of sharp hunger.

"I—I have glutinous rice cakes?"

"Oh!" said the woman in surprise. "That's fine then. Get them out."

The rice cakes were all Dieu had to eat for the next two days, but she figured that her chances for being around in two days' time probably went up if she shared them now. She pulled them one-handed out of her bag, giving them to the woman.

To her surprise, the woman pulled her down to sit next to her in front of the shrine, and let her go, dividing the rice cakes between them.

"You can run away if you like," the woman said callously—

~

"No, she would have said that kindly," rumbled Sinh Hoa, who Chih had thought was sleeping.

"Lady?"

"She wouldn't have been mean about it," said Sinh Hoa sleepily. "It's a courtesy. It's permission. It's being nice."

"I'll remember that," Chih said, and continued.

~

"You can run away if you like," the woman said kindly,

"or you can stay and eat."

Dieu, who had not eaten since daybreak, looked down the long stretch of road and then looked at the rice cakes. Her better judgment told her to run, but her belly told her to get at least one of the rice cakes if she could, and her belly had learned to speak very loudly on her travels.

Dieu tucked her grass traveling shawl a little more snugly around her shoulders, and she nibbled at one of her own rice cakes politely as the woman ate the rest, chewing them with a distracted look on her face. As they ate, Dieu became more aware of the fact that the woman didn't seem to care about the rice cakes at all, and was more interested in looking at Dieu, inspecting her from the top of her wool cap to the toes of her rag-wrapped sandaled feet.

Finally, there was only one rice cake left between them on the stained waxed leaf wrapper, and they both stared at it contemplatively.

"Well," said the woman presently. "Here."

Dieu blinked in surprise as the woman picked up the final rice cake and broke it in two. She examined them with a critical eye, and then she offered the larger of the two pieces to Dieu. Dieu started to reach for it, but then the woman held it up to her lips as if she were a very small child.

Hesitantly, because she wanted to get out of the situation without giving offense and because after all she was very hungry, Dieu opened her mouth and allowed herself to be fed the rice cake.

"Well, that's that," said the woman with satisfaction, climbing to her feet.

Standing, she was shorter than Dieu, coming barely up to Dieu's chin, but she was twice as heavy, if not more. Dieu felt no safer looking down at her than she had sitting and sharing a rice cake with her.

"That's that," echoed Dieu, and the woman nodded without smiling, shutting her eyes for a moment instead.

"My name is Ho Thi Thao. I'll ask for your name when I am sure I want it."

"Will you? Want it, I mean?" asked Dieu in confusion.

"Well, I suppose we'll see. Come along now."

~

"Goodness," said Sinh Loan, looking faintly scandalized. "You mean she didn't know?"

Chih raised their eyebrows at the tiger's tone.

"She knew that she was sitting down with someone that might have eaten her, madam," they said politely.

Sinh Cam shook her ears impatiently.

"She didn't know that Ho Thi Thao was flirting with her! She was being so sweet and romantic, and Scholar

Dieu didn't even *appreciate* it!"

"How so?" asked Chih. They had taken out their writing materials because the tiger was right; if they didn't make it out, the abbey at Singing Hills *would* be fascinated to know this. Maybe they would even get a personal tablet in the hall for the highly esteemed. That was not really a comfort, but it was a nice thought. Now they opened a new page, scooting a little closer to the fire.

"It's the opening to a proper courtship," Sinh Loan said primly. "And our ancestress was a paragon of both decorum and passion. In these lesser days, it's not unknown for a tiger to simply contract a marriage with the first likely looking thing they met on some forest path."

She reached down to tweak Sinh Hoa's tail, making the sleepy tiger grunt and Sinh Cam chuff. The more they talked, Chih realized, the more easy the tigers sounded, the more the threatening rocks were smoothed out of their voices.

"When she shared the food that Scholar Dieu offered her rather than eating it all, she was expressing . . . fond feeling and fascination. When she offered her name without asking for Scholar Dieu's, she was opening the door."

"Opening the door for what?" asked Chih, fascinated in spite of themself.

Sinh Loan waved a thick hand.

"To any number of things. To a courtship. To a single

night of love. To something that would last far longer. To an opportunity to know her more and better. For more."

"To be dinner," Si-yu said with a frown, and Sinh Loan laughed.

"Of course, or do you forbid yourself the privilege of slaying a guest who displeases you at the dinner table?"

Si-yu grumbled, but if she was with the mammoth corps, she knew her history and that was certainly not a privilege that the nobles of the north denied themselves when they decided enough was enough.

"Can you tell us more about the possibilities that Ho Thi Thao was hinting at?" Chih asked. "We know so very little about—"

"That's by design," said Sinh Loan, "but now you know the part about how unwelcome guests and inquiries can be turned into welcome dinners, yes?"

"Yes, I do," said Chih. "Moving on."

Chapter Six

HO THI THAO was a cave dweller like the people who lived in the Painted Cliffs in Anwar, and her cave was a marvel, stretching deep into the mountain. It was an ancient place, lit by a cunning combination of shafts and mirrors. Where those didn't suffice, there were oil lamps scattered throughout, their tricky light showing off low benches scattered with furs and silk cushions, chests overflowing with strings of gold ingots and tablets of jade and turquoise and a royal armory's worth of weapons mounted up on the walls.

"Oh, are these the weapons of your ancestors?" asked Dieu politely.

"No, they're the ones that my ancestors took away from those who would reproach them," said Ho Thi Thao.

Dieu, who after all had studied all her life to be a scholar, recognized some of the weapons on the wall. There was the shield of Wei Lee Lan, who had gone missing some hundred years ago, a pair of matched daggers taken from a captain of the Stinging Nettle Society that went on to become the notorious Sisterhood, and the tiger-killing sword of General Truc Quy. Of course, General Quy had killed tigers until the tigers killed her, and Dieu finally figured out what kind of demon she had followed home.

~

"And what else?" asked Sinh Cam excitedly.

Chih, who had been worried about the line about following the demon home, blinked in surprise.

"What else what?"

"What else did Ho Thi Thao have on her wall? What did she show off to Scholar Dieu?"

"We just have records of those three things, the shield and the daggers and the tiger-killing sword . . ."

"Oh, it's like the tack that the great Ho-shuh was wearing before she and Jo-woon went off to defeat King-Whale," said Si-yu unexpectedly.

She had settled Bao-so as close to the fire as she dared, and she was seated against Piluk's foreleg, Piluk's trunk wrapped around her hand and occasionally swinging it gently.

"Yes?" asked Chih.

"And the storyteller always has to say what Ho-shuh was wearing and where it came from. The stirrups always come from Pari-kie, though, where I'm from."

"Of course they do," said Sinh Loan agreeably. "And of course, Cleric Chih, you should make sure that future tellings of this story mention that Ho Thi Thao had the gloves of the Great Butcher Ik-jee on her wall as well. The Great Butcher was defeated by a tiger from the Boar-backs, you know."

"I will," said Chih, making the notation. If they or their notes made it back to the Singing Hills, the Divine would be very pleased, especially if this shed some light on what had happened to the hunter the north called the Magnificent Ik-jee, who had disappeared without a trace some two hundred years ago.

Everyone settled back into an expectant listening air except for Bao-so, who was unconscious, and Sinh Hoa, who was definitely sleeping. The sky beyond the barn was now entirely black, eating up the shapes of the trees and everything but the faint scatter of snow on the ground, which sparkled in the dim firelight. The cold was sinking into everything, and Chih shrugged a little further into their sheepskin coat, folding their hands into the pockets inside the sleeves.

"The next part is a little odd," they said.

"Oh?" asked Sinh Loan as Sinh Cam buried her nose under her paw with a chuffing sound. If Chih didn't know better, they would have said it was a giggle.

"Yes. The story of the tiger Ho Thi Thao and Scholar Dieu came down to us long after they were both dead, through a traveling actor who told it to a literate friend. The distortion of some fifty years, a natural storyteller, and a monk from Ue County can be immense . . ."

"Well?" said Sinh Loan."

"All right. The text as it was given to me says . . ."

~

So Ho Thi Thao showed Dieu all the treasures she had, ending with her sleeping place. The bed was covered with a lavish embroidered quilt featuring water bison, pronghorn deer, goats, rabbits, and humans, all running, and stretched over the bed as a canopy was the glorious pelt of an enormous tiger.

"And that," she said proudly, "is the skin of my mother, who I killed."

~

Sinh Loan's eyes narrowed and Sinh Cam's head came up in surprise.

~

"Why would you do such a thing?" said Dieu.

"Why, because I wanted what was hers, and because all things are mine. Come here, and let me show you the things I have killed, embroidered on my bed."

Dieu went to listen to the tiger's tales of everything she had killed, and the next morning, the tiger gone hunting, she left without a scratch.

~

"Well," said Sinh Loan, her voice as taut as a zither string. "Is *that* what they say happened?"

"It is," said Chih. They were aware that Si-yu had stood up, her lance in her hands again.

"How awful!" said Sinh Cam, shaking her head. "How could they, that's the *best part* and they ruined it, that's not how it went at all."

Sinh Cam came to her feet, forcing Sinh Loan to sit up in irritation, and she paced back and forth, occasionally biting the cold air as if she wanted to get a bad taste out of her mouth.

"Please tell me how it went instead, lady," Chih said respectfully. "I can only tell the story as it has been told to me."

"Even if it is wrong and wicked?" asked Sinh Loan coldly. "Even if, as you said yourself, you knew it to be imperfect?"

There was a primitive part of Chih's mind that was telling them to run *right now,* but they ignored it. Instead they took a deep breath and then another because Sinh Loan considered them a person and would give them some warning before she killed them. Probably.

"It is the only version of the story I know," Chih said. "Tell me another, and I'll tell that instead."

"Or you will keep them both in your vault and think one is as good as the other," said Sinh Hoa, speaking up unexpectedly, her voice gravelly with sleep. "That's almost worse."

"I can't do anything until you tell me what's wrong, lady," Chih said, and then they shut their mouth.

A complicated sort of three-way communication passed between the tigers. Sinh Loan looked coldly furious; if a tiger could be said to pout Sinh Cam pouted ferociously; and Sinh Hoa looked sleepy, but perhaps that was only how she always looked.

"So, are they going to eat us because of your story?" Si-yu asked. "If it's any consolation, I thought that you told it well so far."

"They might," Chih said, and because they knew the tigers were listening with at least half an ear, "or they may not, and instead tell me the true version."

Finally, Sinh Cam and Sinh Hoa settled to the ground again, and Sinh Loan sat up straight, shoulders square and eyes gleaming in the light.

"All right, cleric. This is told to you in good faith. If we allow you to return to the Singing Hills, I trust that you will tell it there in good faith as well."

~

With the pride of the tiger who had eaten one of the sun's sacred calves, Ho Thi Thao took Scholar Dieu by the hand and led her through her house, pointing out the treasures she had won through longer teeth, sharper claws, and a greater belly than her enemies.

Of all the tigers living in that era, Ho Thi Thao was one of the greatest, proud and hungry, and she had many treasures to show off. It must have been that she already favored Scholar Dieu more than a little because not only did she show her a jar containing the hand bones of a giant and the teeth of the last talking bear in the Boarbacks, she also led her to the deepest parts of her house, so far inside the mountain's heart that only the oil of dead whales lit the way.

Canopied over Ho Thi Thao's bed was the pelt of a great tiger, one almost as large as the scout's calf's there. The paws swung down, still tipped in silvery claws, and the orange was bright and living and the black was deep and dead.

"Who was that?" asked Scholar Dieu, and Thao smiled.

"It is the skin of He Leaps and Leaps, killed by my grandfather in lawful combat," she said. "Some people say that he was only ever a story and that his bones are words and his eyes are laughter, but no. He was real, he was hungry, and now his skin stretches over me like the sky when I sleep."

"And are you worthy of such a thing?" asked Scholar Dieu.

If the words had come from someone less interesting, who smelled less good, who was less beautiful, Ho Thi Thao would have killed them immediately, so insulted she might have left them for lesser things to eat. Instead the words came from Scholar Dieu, and they only made Ho Thi Thao smile.

"Come and see," she said, pulling her beneath the skin of He Leaps and Leaps. "Let me show you."

And so Scholar Dieu stayed in Ho Thi Thao's bed for three nights, and on the morning of the third day, she woke alone, so she dressed and went down the mountain without a single unwanted mark on her body.

~

"Thank you, madam," said Chih, sketching a bow from

their seated position. "I have recorded your story here, and if I return to Singing Hills, it will be copied into the archives."

"Or even if your records return without you," observed Sinh Hoa sleepily.

"You didn't tell it right," Sinh Cam said sulkily, but Sinh Loan ignored her, instead folding her hands neatly on her lap and nodding to Chih.

"Continue."

"Of course, madam."

Chapter Seven

SCHOLAR DIEU CAME DOWN from Wulai Mountain to the banks of the Oanh River. It was broad and wide, placid as a water buffalo except for the places where it bucked and swirled with a secret strange madness. She found at the foot of the mountain a flat-bottomed boat complete with a long pole hitched to one side, but instead of a boatman, there was the tiger resting in the boat, a satisfied look on her face.

Dieu looked left and look right, and the tiger, her eyes half-closed, spoke with Ho Thi Thao's voice.

"There is a bridge five days north, and a proper ferry seven days south," she said. "In case you were wondering."

Dieu bit her lip nervously.

"I have no more food," she said. "I had intended to stop at the village of Nei after the river crossing."

"That's not very interesting to me," the tiger said, and Scholar Dieu resisted the urge to pick up a river stone and to pitch it as hard as she could at the tiger's round face.

"Did you eat the boatman?" she asked, and the tiger opened one eye.

"No, but I could if you wanted me to. He ran off somewhere."

"No, that's not what I want. I want to get across the river."

"If only you had a boat to help you."

"Yes, if only!"

The tiger made as sympathetic a face as a tiger could make.

"It seems I have this boat, little scholar. Why don't you ask me to get you across the river?"

Dieu took a deep breath.

"Please, Ho Thi Thao, will you take me across the river?"

"What will you give me?"

Angrily, Dieu spread her meager possessions out on the bank. It wasn't very much, just a change of clothes and some embroidered cloth slippers, and the few books she could keep back from her family's creditors.

The tiger came to the bank to look over her things carefully, turning her head this way and that. She nosed at the books and the clothes without interest, and finally she shook her head.

"Do you have *nothing* valuable there?"

"But of course I do," said Dieu. "Look, here, this is

Songs of Everlasting Sorrow, the poems that the poet Lu Bi wrote when his wife had gone ahead of him into death."

She paused.

"I could read it to you if you like. If that would be enough payment for getting me across the river."

"Hm. Give me a taste, and if it is good, I will allow you to read the rest. And then I will row this boat across the river with you in it."

Dieu, a little surprised that that had worked at all, knelt on the side of the river and opened the small volume on her lap. She skipped the first quarter, because it was only the praise of the emperor at the time, and she skipped the first few pages of the second quarter, because it was only a description of the land of the dead, which was beautiful in a certain way, but far from enticing.

"And so you came to my house on the soft pads of a midwinter kitten, the whisper of your black tresses sweeping your heels, and so you came to my heart just as quietly. Why, then, did you make such a terrible noise when you let go of my hand and departed, a great trumpeting of horns, a great beating of drums? We had always kept our home in the sweetest of silence, broken only with a dropped spool of scarlet thread or a soft cry from your lips early in the morning. Now your departure crashes like a thunder, and the timbers of the house shake with the force of the space you left behind."

They were Dieu's favorite lines, and she was almost afraid to look up to see how the tiger took them. When you love a thing too much, it is a special kind of pain to show it to others and to see that it is lacking.

The tiger, however, was nodding her head, an expression of great concentration on her round face.

"Yes, that is good. Read me all of that, and then read it to me again, and I will take you across the river."

"I did not say that I would read it twice," Dieu muttered, but quietly, because she read well, and she enjoyed it. "Do you want all of it, or only the part—"

The tiger uttered a low growl, and her eyes took on a peculiar stony hardness, like jade or carnelian, nothing living at all, but very bright.

"I want all of it," she insisted, "and I want it twice."

"Very well," said Dieu, and she opened her book from the beginning and as the tiger listened, she read it through twice. On the second pass, the tiger murmured the words with her, almost perfectly, and then she recited the whole of the poem from memory, perfect in tone as if she could read herself.

"All right," she said finally. "Come sit in the boat, and I will row you across the river."

~

Chih paused.

"So how was that?" they asked, and the tigers thought for a moment. At least, Sinh Loan and Sinh Cam thought. Sinh Hoa was probably asleep, though at this point, Chih would not have bet a great deal of money on it.

"Good," Sinh Cam said. "That is how we tell it, mostly. But why did Ho Thi Thao not eat the boatman? It's a much better idea than just driving him off."

"Because it is not such a good story for humans if they get randomly eaten and do not deserve it," said Sinh Loan, somewhat to Chih's surprise. "I suppose they mostly tell this story to humans after all."

"It's still different from what we would say," said Sinh Hoa, her eyes closed.

"What would you say?" asked Si-yu abruptly.

Chih glanced at her in surprise. The mammoth scout looked a little calmer at least, and she looked from Chih to the tigers and back again, as if unsure which story she should trust, if either.

Sinh Loan yawned, shrugging her thick shoulders.

"The big difference is that Ho Thi Thao eats her book after she has the story twice."

Once, Chih sat very still in an Ue County graveyard pretending to be a junior ghost so they could hear the stories that the corpses rose to tell each other at the Rose Moon festival. If they had been caught, they would have been torn from limb to limb, but if they had heard of such a thing from the corpses, there was a good chance that they would have done exactly what they did now, which was gasp and stare.

"*Why* would she do such a thing?" Chih demanded, and then they covered their mouth with their hand, blushing red.

Sinh Loan smiled triumphantly as if she had caught Chih out. In a very real way, she had. Chih had spent years at Singing Hills perfecting an open face and a listening posture, and being startled to gasps and stares was something that was only meant to happen to very young clerics.

"Scholar Dieu asked the same thing," Sinh Loan said. "Here."

~

As the sun grew ripe and started to drop towards the horizon, Scholar Dieu read the poem, and as she did, it came to Ho Thi Thao how very beautiful she was. She had been beautiful in bed for three nights, which was important, and she was beautiful now, when she was angry at having her way blocked. It came to Ho Thi Thao that perhaps she wanted to learn how else the scholar was beautiful, and even in what ways the scholar might be ugly, which could also be fascinating and beloved.

She let the scholar's voice lull her into a half-dream as the boat rocked in the river's waves, and then, too soon, she closed the book and stood up.

"I have paid my fee, and now you should hold up your end of the bargain," she said.

"Of course. Give me the book."

The scholar did, and as my sister said, she gutted it with one stroke of her paw and swallowed the wounded pages in two great bites.

Then Dieu stood up, crying out in pain as if she were the one who had been clawed, and when she stamped her foot, the river itself shook in its banks, so great was her anger.

"Why did you do that?" she demanded, tears falling down her face, and Ho Thi Thao looked at her in puzzlement.

"I told you I wanted it," she said, "and now it is mine."

In response, Scholar Dieu scooped up a rock from the river bank and pitched it as hard as she could at poor Ho Thi Thao, flung so hard that it chipped one of her magnificent fangs.

"And so that is yours too," Scholar Dieu said angrily. "Now fulfill your bargain and take me across the river."

For a moment, the pain in Ho Thi Thao's tooth made her want to strike the scholar's head from her shoulders, but then the word came to her, the way words seldom did, *beautiful,* and the scholar was.

Instead of killing her, Ho Thi Thao only bowed her head humbly and went into her human form, which could grasp the oars and row as skillfully as any river man.

They were silent as they crossed the Oanh River, and when they came to the opposite side, Dieu gathered up her things and stalked away from the riverbank without a backwards look, taking Ho Thi Thao's eyes with her.

~

Chih cleared their throat.

"Yes, metaphorically," said Sinh Loan with great patience.

Chih nodded, making another note. In some of the Rose Moon ghoul stories they had heard, it wouldn't have been.

"All right. So after Dieu walked away from the river, she came to the house of the Cheng clan of western Zhou."

Chapter Eight

THE CHENG CLAN OF western Zhou was a long way from western Zhou.

They had been driven out for supporting the wrong prince, who had at the time seemed like the most righteous son of the previous Zhou emperor and a fairly good bet considering his mother was backed by the Ki clan. Unfortunately, his brother had turned out to be more righteous instead, and also a little handier with a great deal of bear gall poison.

So the Cheng clan fell into some chaos, and what was left of them fled to the hinterlands, purchased a mansion in the heart of a haunted forest, and allowed the ghosts and ghouls and monsters to defend them as righteousness, propriety, and a fully armed house guard could not.

Relying on the protection of ghouls and monsters is as poor an idea as backing the least righteous of an emperor's sons, and eventually, the Cheng family learned that, though a little too late.

Of course, Dieu knew none of that when she came to their gates just as the sun was setting. She had been aware all day of the tiger behind her, following at what she imagined was a respectful distance and clumsy in her fascination, but the scholar paid her no mind.

Instead, she rang the iron bell at the Chengs' sturdy door, and when she told the old doorman that she was a prospective candidate for the examinations in Ahnfi, she was ushered in and the door closed quickly behind her.

At the time, the Cheng family was the old patriarch who had served the previous emperor, his first wife, his second wife, his second son, and his baby daughter. They had been more numerous not long ago, and Dieu made it her business not to prod at the holes in their family. Instead, she came to kneel neatly at the table with them as they served her all manner of delicacies from their home, fileted pieces of pheasant fanned out and drizzled with yuzu and ginger, lucky whole fish arranged on the plate with a scatter of salt as if it were swimming, and slivers of a pig's heart soaked in yogurt and fried in sesame oil. They set in front of her a bowl of pure white rice dusted with ruby salt and sesame seeds, and to her left was a bowl of soup so clear she could see the figure of a fox running at the bottom of the bowl, and to her right, there was a pair of jade chopsticks, bound at the crown by a delicate gold chain.

It was a feast fit to honor a princess, all rolled out for a rather tattered scholar, but Dieu was so hungry that she simply ate the food that was put in front of her. She had never eaten so well in her life, and as she ate, the Cheng patriarch nodded wisely at the head of the table as his two wives kept up a stream of witty entertaining talk, lively and clever as if they had never left court.

Dieu was almost full when she noticed the little dish of hawthorn berries next to the littlest girl. The red berries gleamed, sprinkled with large crystals of rock sugar, and as Dieu watched, the little girl reached out to pop two in her mouth, swallowing them happily. She caught Dieu watching her, and she scooped up two more, offering them bashfully.

"Here," she said. "You have some too."

Her first instinct was to pop them into her mouth, but then an image of the house she had left came to mind, of the hawthorn tree that grew fifteen paces from her door. She had left before the tree burst into leaves, let alone flowers or berries, and the beautiful red berries were autumn-ripe, full to bursting with tart juice and slightly soft under her fingers.

"Ah," she said, and then she looked down at the rest of the food on the table. Ptarmigan lived in these woods but pheasant was rarer, and sea bass certainly did not swim in the rivers. Suddenly she realized that the eyes of all the family were upon her.

"Why don't you eat?" asked Patriarch Cheng's second

wife. "You'll teach little Jia to be wary of the generosity of strangers if you do not."

"Actually, there are quite a few aphorisms that tell us we should not take advantage of our hosts' good will," Dieu said. "Here, I could read us a few . . ."

She reached for her bag, knowing she was babbling, but in her bag were the paper talismans that her tutor had insisted she purchase. Before she could get her hand into her things, however, the second son, who was very handsome with eyebrows like dark charcoal and a face as pale and pretty as a maiden's, placed his hand over hers.

"Oh, but won't you keep quiet, keep quiet while I drink in your beauty?" he asked, and his eyes were very dark.

Dieu was very still.

"Yes," said the second wife encouragingly. "Keep quiet, keep quiet and stay with us. We will feed you all the food that you like best and let you sleep over linen and under silk."

"Stay with us," said the first wife graciously. "Keep quiet, keep quiet and marry our son, who is not so bad for being the child of a second wife, and give us a baby boy to lighten our hall with laughter."

"Oh, I don't think so," said Dieu, who knew she would make an even worse wife and mother than she would an imperial official, and she tried to rise, but the second son had not let go of her hand. Now little Jia had stood up on her opposite side and as she was trying to pull away, the little girl popped a hawthorn berry in her mouth, so fast and determined that Dieu swallowed it before she could figure out what had passed.

Oh . . . oh the seeds are poisonous, she thought vaguely, and then she rose and followed the second son through the mansion to his rooms at the rear.

How strange it was, she thought, that the walls of such a well-to-do family were so dark and spangled with mold, and how very odd it was that she kicked up all manner of worms and insects as she walked through the halls.

"Don't worry about those," said the second son. "My room is soft and warm and if you keep quiet, keep quiet, you can stay there forever."

Then he opened the door to his bedroom and for a moment, she saw a sad and sunken grave, the center hollowed out, and the thought came to her, with the calm that barely masks hysteria, *Oh, I shall have to be on top,* and then her vision blurred and it was only the softest-looking bed she had ever seen, with long gauze curtains in silk that were embroidered with—

They were meant to be embroidered with spells to keep out peeping ghouls and wights, but when Dieu tilted her head around, she could see that they were nothing of the sort. At first she thought that there was simply a stroke or two missing, which might have been a disaster, but common enough, but then she realized that there was something wrong, very wrong with the entire line, and perhaps the entire stanza, and her hand shot out to grab at the gauze.

"Wait, I know this one, it's not right..." she said, and then because she was not a graceful woman, she pulled too hard and dragged the silk drapes down on herself and her new bridegroom, but the drapes in her hands were moldy cotton rotted through, the bed was a grave after all, her bridegroom—

Oh—oh that's a corpse, that's a dead person, and he has been dead for some time because his hair has fallen out and his teeth have fallen out and something is sitting where his eyes used to be, but I do not know what it is...

She opened her mouth to scream, but then the iron bell above the door rang, and he was a handsome young man who smelled of camellia oil again, except now she knew he was actually—or perhaps also—a corpse, and he smiled at her reassuringly.

"It is only a guest come to call," he said. "Never worry, my dearest, my darling."

"We—we should go see who it is," she managed, her throat dry. "We should not start our marriage by dishonoring our guests."

She could see him hesitate, could almost see him wondering whether it would be better to simply push her into the grave and wrap his sinew-strung arms around her, but that wasn't the game, she realized. If she was a bride, then he was a groom, and not a horror. If she was civil, then so must he be.

He smiled, showing perfect white teeth, and nodded.

"Then let us see who is at the door," he said.

By the time they returned to the banqueting hall, Ho Thi Thao was already there, stretched out casually at the place that Dieu had just vacated, her bare feet dirty on the clean floors as she picked through the fileted pheasant with one idle finger. The Cheng family looked frozen where they sat, the patriarch especially, with his face as foolish as a carved turnip.

"Ah, there you are," she said. "I came to see how you were doing."

Dieu took a deep breath. Tiger or corpse, it should have been a harder choice, but of course it wasn't.

"I need help," she said, and when the dead second son of the Cheng family's hand tightened on hers, a low growl from the tiger made him step away entirely.

"Do you?" asked the tiger. "None of your other books looked very interesting."

"I—I have some money left, and—and some talismans that could . . ."

"No, not very interesting at all," said the tiger.

"You could take my name," suggested Dieu, and the tiger wrinkled her nose.

"And what good is that to me?"

The corpses looked between one and the other, and Dieu's skin tried to crawl off her body. She shuddered.

"You could ... you could have my hair," she offered, remembering how taken the tiger had been with the wife's black hair in *Songs of Everlasting Sorrow*. "It doesn't sweep my heels, but it's pretty."

"I like it better on your head," said the tiger. "Maybe try again before I get bored."

Dieu swallowed hard, and then something came to her. She no longer had *Songs of Everlasting Sorrow*, but it had been her favorite, and it lived in her mind and in her heart still.

"From the deepest part of the Yellow Springs, my dear husband, I call to you ..."

"I'm right here," said the second Cheng son in surprise, and the tiger growled.

"No one was talking to you," she said.

"My eyes are open for always, my mouth is empty for always, and always will my soul reach for yours. In the land of the dead, there are only blackbirds, and I send this one to you, in the hopes that you remember me still. Light me a stick of incense, and so long as it burns, let me sit in the chamber outside your bedroom again. Until it goes out ..."

"Let me stay and be for you," said the tiger, and she rose and drove away the ghosts of the Cheng mansion.

~

"Oh!" said Sinh Cam, her eyes wide. "Oh, I *like* that! Say the verse again, the last part."

Chih opened their mouth to comply, but Sinh Loan was shaking her head.

"Abysmal, cleric, completely abysmal. That's not what happened at all."

"No, but I like it *more*," Sinh Cam said enthusiastically. "The verse was—oh!"

She yowled in offense when Sinh Loan reached out to cuff her ear.

"You're not supposed to like that," she scolded. "It's *wrong.*"

Sinh Cam licked her paw and groomed her affronted ear vigorously.

"I can like it if I want," she said sullenly.

"You can, but quietly, or the cleric will think it is all right to keep telling it that way."

"They can tell both," said Sinh Cam imperiously, and then Sinh Hoa, newly awakened by the fuss, wrapped a large paw over Sinh Cam's shoulder and started grooming her drowsily.

"They can't until they're told the right version," Sinh Hoa mumbled. "Elder sister?"

"Of course," said Sinh Loan with dignity.

~

Ho Thi Thao's mouth ached, but she could still smell Dieu's anger, which was delicious to her, and so she followed her all the way into the forest, making sure to crack sticks and kick stones as she went because how else would Dieu know that she was there?

She was to the edge of her claimed territory now, and though simply being in a place meant that it was her territory, she did not know right away that Scholar Dieu had chosen to stop at a fox's barrow.

The Cheng family of western Zhou had settled there, exiled and unlucky, and they were devoured in less than a year's time by the local foxes, who were more than happy to move in afterwards and help themselves to the Chengs' house, their fine Zhou manners, their clothes, and of course their skulls. The Cheng patriarch had been killed by soldiers, but they made do instead with a carved turnip stuck on a stick. When the old man was called upon to nod with grave dignity or shake his head with disapproval, one of the nearby foxes would reach out and jiggle the stick appropriately.

All of this Ho Thi Thao saw when she knocked down the gate, and then she was walking into the banqueting hall, where the mother fox sat with her turnip-head husband, her sister, and her cubs by her side. Their table was a rotted well cover, and arranged upon it was the offal that foxes like best to eat, half-rotted moles, moldy purple yams, and piles of termite grubs, dug out from under dead trees.

Ho Thi Thao did not care about any of that. What she did care about was Scholar Dieu, sitting beside the eldest fox cub, her head draped with a decayed white shroud to serve as a bride's headdress.

"Well, it looks like a wedding," she said with some surprise, for she had not thought that Scholar Dieu reckoned her affections so lightly.

"It is, and you are not invited," snapped the mother fox.

"I'm a tiger, I am invited wherever I care to go," replied Ho Thi Thao.

"I'm inviting her," said Dieu unexpectedly, and she rose from her bridegroom's side to take Ho Thi Thao's arm.

When she sat down at the table, she could see that there were three small cups of rice wine—real rice wine, because foxes do have *some* manners—in front of Dieu. She had drunk two of them, and if she drank the third, then there would be nothing even a tiger could do, for then she would be married to the fox barrow, and nothing could change that.

"I want to leave now," said Dieu, impressively calm in spite of her fate. "Can you help me?"

"I could," said Ho Thi Thao, still a little stung by how fast Dieu had found a husband. "What will you give me?"

"My hair," said Dieu, who remembered how Ho Thi Thao had stroked it over and over again on that first night.

"I like it best on your head, so no," said Ho Thi Thao.

"I'll give you my right hand, then," said Dieu, thinking of their second night.

"It would only be a single bite, and again, it works best attached to you. So, no."

Ho Thi Thao considered.

"Give me that little green chip you wear around your neck. I see you playing with it all the time, give me that."

To her surprise, Dieu shook her head.

"I can't give it to you," she said, and Ho Thi Thao became very angry.

"Then it sounds to me that you would like to stay here and marry the fox cub," Ho Thi Thao snapped. "Fine."

She stood up to go, but Dieu held her back.

"If you bring me out of this place, I will share every meal that I ever have with you. I will let you eat first from every dish and drink first from every cup."

When she said that, you might have knocked Ho Thi Thao over with a feather, and her heart beat like the hunting drums of the great Kieu clan, and her eyes were as wide as the moon pools in the deepest forest.

"Oh," she said. *"Oh."*

"You can't do that!" complained the oldest fox sister. "Everyone knows tigers are bad-tempered gamblers who will beat you!"

"She'll make you watch her cubs while she goes to carouse at the floating ghost palaces," said the younger. "She'll leave you alone all the time, and a fox would never do that to you."

The turnip-head patriarch was shaken in vigorous agreement, but the son only looked on nervously because he had few illusions about what kind of husband he would be, and even fewer about how well he would fare against a tiger in a matrimonial duel.

"Do you mean what you said?" demanded Ho Thi Thao, and when Dieu nodded, the tiger reached over to pull the shroud off her head.

"All right," she said. "Close your eyes."

Scholar Dieu did as she was told, and so she only heard and did not see the foxes' murder, not how the smallest cub was eaten whole or how the adult sisters had their backs broken before their heads were snapped off.

Their son escaped and went off to make some trouble for the tiger of the Carcanet Mountains, but that is, of course, another story.

Ho Thi Thao was sensitive and did not want to scandalize her new bride with so much blood. Though Dieu's clothes were splattered with blood and her shoes quite ruined, Ho Thi Thao was pleased to see that the scholar's eyes were still tightly closed, even if she shivered like a pine tree in the strong wind.

"All right," she said. "Come on, and I will find us a better place to sleep than this."

She led Scholar Dieu out of the foxes' grave, bringing her to a soft place under a spreading red pine, and there she took off Dieu's clothes and shoes because they were of course ruined. After that, she hunted for them a fat piglet and allowed Dieu to singe it as she liked best, taking the best pieces that were her due from her new wife's pretty fingers.

~

"I like this one better," said, of all people, Si-yu.

"I don't care for food that flatters," said Sinh Loan coolly, but Si-yu shook her head.

"And I don't care about poetry. It's nice, but . . . the first bite of every meal that Dieu eats? That's good. That's how the old warriors who don't like to use words like *love* talk. My grandfather still says *I will always give you the first bite of my dinner, you terrible woman,* to my grandmother. I didn't know that tigers said it too."

"You must have gotten it from us," Sinh Loan said with some stiff pride. "That's something that tigers say, and—yes, cleric? You look puzzled."

"So at this point in the story, Scholar Dieu is *married* to the tiger?"

"Of course she is. In fact, she was the one who proposed, and that is what makes her betrayal later even more serious."

"She couldn't have known that that was what she was doing," Chih protested. "She wasn't a tiger, she didn't grow up close to tigers. She knew the classics and she could compose original poetry and recite from the great books, but—"

"Well, what else does it mean when someone offers to share every meal with you, and to let you eat and drink from their very plate?" asked Sinh Cam practically, and Chih paused.

"There are more answers to that than you may think," Chih temporized, because there were, but they could see that there was only one answer that really mattered to tigers. They made the appropriate notations.

The temperature had dropped again, and the snow was

falling more steadily. Chih stood up to stretch and to feed the fire, and as they did so, Sinh Hoa padded off into the darkness. In a surprisingly short amount of time, she returned with the skinny carcass of a fresh-killed white hare. It would barely be a bite for a tiger, but she tore out the belly with a near-surgical precision and came to drop it into Chih's hands.

"Eat," the tiger said graciously. "It's hardly our custom to starve people telling us stories."

Chih fought back the urge to ask if this meant that they would be legally or by tradition bound to the tiger sisters. If they were, they would just have to figure it out later.

Si-yu took the hare from Chih, and before she skinned it, she pulled out the entrails and cut out the tiny heart and the somewhat larger liver, holding them out to Chih.

"Pick one," she said, "I'll take the other."

Fascinated, Chih picked the heart, and when Si-yu popped the liver in her mouth, they did the same with the heart.

Most importantly, the heart was still warm, and Chih's sharp teeth cut neatly through the stiff muscle, making it a little easier to chew. It tasted mostly of iron and blood, things they weren't really used to, but after fighting back an urge to gag, they swallowed quickly, feeling an almost dizzying rush of warmth and satisfaction. It had been hours since the reindeer meat from that afternoon, and it would be a while yet until dawn.

"And now we're married," Si-yu said solemnly, and Chih jumped for a moment, shooting her an exasperated look as she laughed.

"You could be more serious about all of this," they said, and Si-yu shrugged.

"They said that they would let Piluk go if worst came to worst, Bao-so's still breathing, and they're not going to eat us until your story is over. What've I got to be afraid of now?"

"Making fun of our marital traditions?" suggested Sinh Loan.

"I'm making fun of mine, it's fine," Si-yu retorted, and Chih was beginning to see perhaps why Si-yu's family had been in the mammoth corps for two hundred years. It probably wasn't safe to have them out of it.

The tigers waited patiently as Si-yu cooked the rabbit in a pot over the fire, waited patiently even when Si-yu and Chih ate, and were only a little restless when Si-yu went make sure that Piluk was as comforted as she could be. Piluk seemed to be restless, her trunk swaying back and forth, her head lowered. Her small black eyes seemed to squint at something that Chih couldn't see, and on occasion, she grumbled, her mouth shut but working fiercely. When Si-yu offered her a handful of fodder from the trough, she turned it away entirely, making the scout frown.

"She's nervous," she said. "She's almost never off her feed."

"I wonder why?" asked Sinh Loan innocently, and Si-yu glared.

Finally, there was no more stalling, and Chih sat back down by the fire to continue.

Chapter Nine

THE TIGER WAS GLUTTED from her slaughter of the vengeful ghosts of the Cheng clan, and so she did not stir when Scholar Dieu left in the morning.

She continued on her way to Ahnfi, and now the roads grew wider and broader and a little safer. She traveled for a while with some tightrope walkers and tumblers, and then with a young woman with wide eyes painted on her eyelids who felt the lumps on Dieu's head and predicted for her a future of strange beds but good sex. Then she suggested that the bed upstairs at the inn might be sufficiently strange, which Dieu politely declined, because life was complicated enough.

It certainly wasn't made easier by the tiger that she quickly realized was following her. The tiger could not be as bold as she had been in the mountains or the forests. Now she had to follow Dieu in her human shape, walking on two legs instead of four and eating as humans did.

She did not come to speak with Dieu, though more often than not, Dieu would wake up with some singed bit of meat or another by her pillow, wrapped in leaves and left for her just before she rose. Dieu realized with some dismay that the tiger was in love with her, as much as any savage beast could be, and the thought filled her with dread.

She hoped that the tiger would grow bored as the days passed, or perhaps that she would become distressed by the cultivated lands of the south and the presence of soldiers and hunters and magic-workers. Sometimes, the tiger would be quiet for days, but just when Dieu felt some kind of relief, she would catch a glimpse of orange out of the corner of her eye or she would hear a soft chuffing as she woke up to another gift of charred rabbit or cracked and fire-roasted marrow bones.

The tiger did nothing, and as they passed through the triple gates of Ahnfi to the capital itself, she had a moment of terror for the tiger in such a place.

The capital in those days was the last remaining bastion of the Ku Dynasty, their sunset glory, the tomb for their dying sorcery. It was the last place in the falling empire where you could hear the songs of the Midu singers who asked the gods to give them second mouths in their throats, and where you might have your fortune told by the hunted impenetrable Kang Lan sect, who split open stones to read the veins of crystal and nodes of ore found inside them. Ahnfi's lion banners snapped in the air like the fingers of nobles calling for this death or that delicacy, and from the barred windows of the flower and water district, beauties from all over the world plotted, schemed, and gave rise to a thousand stories of death and ambition.

It was impossible to tell whether Ahnfi was breathing its last or whether it would rise up again, either on its own or supported like skin over new and foreign bones. The city and its fate whirled like the skirts of a dancing boy, and through it all, Dieu knew that a tiger was stalking her.

Dieu's heart might have quivered at the idea of entering the Hall of Ferocious Jade, but she had indeed been studying the classics and the lessons of the past for eighteen years. She knew more than just the law of the land, she knew the written law of the heavens, and they were emphatic—people had their place, and so did the beasts.

The emperor lived in his palace, the merchant lived in the storehouse, the farmer lived in the field, the scholar lived in the halls of knowledge, and the corpse lived in the grave. The animals the law called friendly—the rooster, the cow, the dog, and the sheep—lived in the world of men, whether it was a palace or a barn. The animals the law considered wild lived in the forest or the mountain. There were animals that were considered equivocal, like cats and goats and rabbits, but there could be no mistake when it came to a tiger.

Eventually, Dieu thought, the tiger would do something terrible. She would kill a child as she had killed the youngest ghost, or she would decide that some dignitary's pavilion or worse, his wife, was her territory. Then...

Dieu knew that it was only correct that a wild animal should be killed for crossing into territory declared forbidden to her, but after all, the tiger had saved her life.

Dieu made a decision, and with the last of the money she had, she rented a room in a well-appointed tea house, and had them butcher for her four fat piglets. Instead of having them cooked, she only had them dressed in savory herbs and she herself poured their blood onto the doorstep.

As the sun set on Ahnfi, and they lit the first lanterns against the haunted night, the tiger appeared, looking around in appreciation.

"Well, I suppose there is something to be said for living in the city," she said, and she allowed Dieu to bring her to the table and to cut with her own hands small slices of meat from the backs and bellies of the piglets and to drop them right into the tiger's mouth.

There was a clever boy to strum his moon guitar behind a screen, and the tiger fell back on silk cushions, refusing to feed herself and nudging Dieu's hands until she fed her more. Dieu smiled, ignoring the blood that stained the edges of her sleeves, and fed the tiger until there were only bones left on the table, and the tiger was stuffed full, her head on Dieu's lap.

"We'll stay in the city a year," the tiger said drowsily. "And then we shall spend a year in the mountains and decide between us which we like best . . ."

Dieu said nothing, and she slid her fingers around the tiger's wrist, feeling the tiger's pulse grow slower.

Finally, the tiger was asleep, and the boy with the moon guitar came out to look her over.

"Well, that was enough poppy to bring down a mammoth calf," he said.

"You mustn't hurt her," Dieu said anxiously. "She has killed no one—well, no one since coming to the city. She has done nothing wrong . . ."

"I would as soon throw myself into the bear pit," snorted the clever boy, who would one day become the famous Inspector Wen Jilong. "No, we're going to cage her and transport her down the coast."

"Oh," said Dieu. "And she'll be safe there?"

The boy gave her a strange look.

"Well, she'll no longer be in the city, so we'll be safe from her. And when she wakes up in Lanling, she'll probably level at least a district before she gets away, and everyone knows that Lanling has no archers or hunters of note. She'll be fine."

Before Dieu could respond to that, men came to secure the tiger with talismans and chains, and then she was alone with only an official letter of thanks for her service to Ahnfi and some very-well-gnawed pork bones.

~

Chih paused.

"If Dieu was meant to offer the first bites of her food to Ho Thi Thao, I suppose it makes sense that Ho Thi Thao never suspected her . . ."

To their surprise, Sinh Loan was watching her with a nearly indulgent expression on her face.

"Surely you know how silly your story is?"

"I am telling it to you as it was told to me," Chih said. "It has never been my habit to tell someone that their story is silly."

"But you never questioned it? Not once?"

"It was told to me when I was very young. We question those stories less."

"So question it now," said Sinh Loan, taking a tone a bit like that of Cleric Ruzhao, who taught the fourth and fifth year acolytes. However, Cleric Ruzhao had only made them write extra lines when they found themselves on the wrong path. Sinh Loan might do something much worse.

As Chih thought, Sinh Cam's long tail swished back

and forth, and she dropped her chin down to her front paws.

"I can smell that you are confused and worried," the youngest sister said proudly. "I can smell that the scout has a lover among the miners of Suying. I can smell that the mammoth wishes she could sleep but feels that she must keep an eye on things . . ."

"And Ho Thi Thao could certainly smell enough poppy to knock out a mammoth calf," Si-yu said. "She must have known exactly what it was that Dieu was feeding her."

"Oh . . ." Chih considered. "Then I suppose she was very in love with Dieu."

Sinh Loan clapped her hands once in disapproval.

"And what would that mean in the sad little story that you told?" she demanded. "That a great tiger like Ho Thi Thao had grown so heartsick for a skinny little poetry-reading scholar that she would allow herself to be drugged like a water buffalo? That she reckoned her love so cheap that it could be sent to Lanling to terrorize some dockworkers? What does *that* say?"

"That it was a story told by humans who never heard it from a tiger, madam," said Chih, and they sat and waited.

Sinh Loan glared at them, and then with great dignity, she sat up straight.

"Very well. But believe me, if this story is told to me

like that a second time, I will not wait to hear more, and I will certainly eat the teller."

Chih wanted to say something about the fact that stories took longer than that to spread, but then Sinh Loan was speaking again, her voice falling into the easy sway of an elder sister entertaining her siblings with her stories.

~

Ho Thi Thao spent a week with Scholar Dieu under the branches of the red pine tree, but one morning, she found that the scholar had washed her clothes clean of fox's blood and dressed herself again. It had only been a week, but she looked strange in her clothes again, and Ho Thi Thao was not sure she cared for it.

"Take those off," she tried. "Come back here, and I will cook you rabbit just as you like it, and after you have fed me, I will feed you until you are sleepy and ready for me to kiss you again."

"I can't," Dieu said regretfully. "I need to go to Ahnfi."

"Ah," said the tiger. "Then I will go with you."

She followed the scholar all the way to Ahnfi, the city of cages by the sea. Ahnfi was the child of Pan'er, which sunk beneath the waves, and the latter-day daughter of that great city lacked all of the parent's grace and beauty. Instead Ahnfi smelled like ten thousand people in one place, applying peony oil to their bodies to mask their smells and lighting whale-oil lamps in their windows to hold back the honest night. There were a thousand thousand things to eat in Ahnfi, everything from sheep to horse to cavy to beaver, but Ho Thi Thao did not think she could eat a bite without getting a mouthful of the unsavory taste underneath, something that told her that this place was dying and that the rebirth would not come easy.

Together they came to a house that smelled of good tea and mild treachery, and Ho Thi Thao allowed Dieu to settle her there. The four piglets that the frightened servants brought to their table were more than satisfactory, and Ho Thi Thao gorged herself pleasantly on the food from her pretty wife's hands, well-satisfied with the world.

"We'll stay in the city a year," she said, "and then I will take you back to the mountains for a year. After that, we should know which we like better, but I can tell right now that it will be the mountains."

The scholar, however, was a nervous bride, and one still unused to the way of tigers. Perhaps she looked at Ho Thi Thao's sharp claws and was afraid, or perhaps she considered Ho Thi Thao's wicked teeth and wondered.

No matter what the reason, the next day, Ho Thi Thao woke alone, and instead of the wife she had gone to bed with, there was only a simpering creature who shook like a winter leaf as she knelt at the door to the room.

"Your wife has paid for the room," she said, her voice soft and wobbling. "You will be fed and honored as is your right—"

"But where is she?" demanded Ho Thi Thao, and the woman shook her head.

"She has gone to register for the examinations at the Hall of Ferocious Jade," said the woman, her tone faltering. As she grew angrier, it was harder and harder for Ho Thi Thao to look like a human. She grew larger and sharper, and her speech had more growls than words.

"And she did not leave me anything to eat? She did not care to wake me to see her off?"

The woman groaned at that, the noise so irritating that Ho Thi Thao killed her with a single bound, breaking the woman's neck and cutting off that awful sound.

That should have been breakfast, but Ho Thi Thao growled with fury. She would only eat if Dieu fed her, and Dieu was nowhere to be found. The woman she had killed lay at her feet, and in a fury, Ho Thi Thao stepped over her and walked out into the city, looking for her wife.

Chapter Ten

CHIH SHIVERED, and it was not just because of the cold. They had stoked the fire up, but it was doing them less good against the night. They were sat as close to it as they dared, and Si-yu was pressed close to them, holding Bao-so close on her other side.

Sinh Loan smiled coldly.

"Does it frighten you to think of what a hungry tiger might do in a city like Ahnfi-that-was?" she asked. "Are you thinking of all the people she might have killed?"

"Yes," Chih said. They had been taught that where a professional demeanor and inquisitiveness could not be found, honesty would have to serve. "Ho Thi Thao was angry, and she was offended. Ahnfi was the greatest city of the age, and she could not have gone five steps beyond the door without meeting someone else to hurt."

Sinh Cam shook her head.

"No, she wasn't offended, or she wasn't *just* offended. She was heartbroken."

"And she was going to take it out on every human that

crossed her path?" asked Si-yu with some indignation. "That's terrible."

"What did you do the last time you got your heart broken?" asked Sinh Cam practically.

"Shouted a lot! Signed up for every long patrol I qualified for, and made a nuisance of myself to whoever was assigned to ride it with me. Brushed Piluk until there was enough wool to felt up a coat for my baby cousin. I didn't kill people."

"But perhaps you wanted to?" asked Sinh Cam, and there was something earnest in her voice.

Si-yu hesitated, and Chih watched, fascinated.

"She broke up with me and took an Ingrusk posting without letting me explain," Si-yu said finally. "Maybe."

"But you wouldn't," said Sinh Cam. "And I wouldn't. And Ho Thi Thao probably didn't, either."

"She did," Sinh Loan said stiffly. "Of course she did."

"In all fairness, elder sister, she likely didn't," said Sinh Hoa. "If she had, they would still have her skull hung up over the gate in Anh. She didn't."

"Of course she did," Sinh Loan said, and she turned her hard gaze to Chih. "Cleric, make sure you note the story as I have told it to you, and not as my young and foolish sisters have done."

Chih nodded, because that was what footnotes were for. They let out a deep breath, watching the plume of steam roll out in front of the firelight. They were so tired that they were shaking, and their eyes watered copiously.

"Shall I continue?" they asked.

Sinh Hoa went back to sleep, Sinh Cam nodded eagerly, and Sinh Loan, after a long moment, gestured her assent with a wave of her broad hand.

~

After that, there was nothing for Dieu to do but to prepare for her exams. Now that she was in the city, she was the closest she had ever been to the imperial scholars whose ranks she was hoping to join. She saw two of them on the street in their sheltered oxcarts, and when their two entourages met, a great shouting went up. None shouted louder than the two honored scholars themselves, dressed in the red robes lined with black that were their right to wear, flapping their long sleeves like indignant roosters.

They struck her as being very like roosters, ready to kick the other to death for the matter of a few grubs or right of way on the thoroughfare. She tried to imagine what she herself might look like dressed in red and shouting in the street, and she couldn't do it, or perhaps, she didn't want to do it.

When Dieu finally came to the Hall of Ferocious Jade,

she felt like she was entering the mouth of a tiger's cave, and it did not escape her awareness that she had done just that without this amount of fear and nerves.

This is what I am meant to do, Dieu thought, pushing away her thoughts of roosters and tigers.

She was the last prospective scholar to enter. Another turn of the water-clock, and the door would have been barred to her, not to open again for another four years.

She was met at the door by a gaunt-faced man in the examiners' dark orange robes, and he took in her travel clothes and her ragged appearance with a carefully but not perfectly concealed disdain. He examined her jade chip under a series of stacked lenses, and it seemed to Dieu that he was disappointed to find that it was not a fraud. He had no reason to have her driven off by the dogs that waited beside him, and so he returned the chip to her hand and asked her the three questions that every scholar entering the hall had to answer.

Dieu of course, knew the questions by heart, just as she knew that she needed to answer yes to each one to be allowed entry. They were, as her tutor had said, the easiest questions she would be asked, so she should take the time to savor them before what came next.

The examiner at the gate did not bother rising from his desk, and he gave her a weary look. He had likely asked these questions eighty times that day alone.

"Do you enter the Hall of Ferocious Jade willingly and with no coercion?"

"Yes," Dieu said, because it was true. There was no family behind her that had tacked her braid to the wall behind her to stop her head from drooping over her books in weariness. There was no lover held hostage until she emerged from the Hall with winning marks. She stood at the gates because of nothing but her own will.

"Do you swear to honor the rules of the Hall of Ferocious Jade?"

"Yes," Dieu responded, because she did not want to be killed by the examiners or the angry ghosts of past scholars for the suspicion of cheating. The examiners could be reasoned with, perhaps even, if the whispers were true, bribed, but the dead students, not at all.

"If you come out from the examinations a triumph, do you accept your place in the heavens of the empire, underneath the authority and protection of the emperor and the nobles?"

Dieu started to say *yes*, and then abruptly, she realized that she could not, not honestly. In her head, she thought of the constellation that she lived and moved in, the one that she had accepted, the one under which she slept and the one to which her heart had already been given, and there was no emperor involved. There was only a flash of orange and black, the slow blink of eyes like jade.

"No," she said to her own surprise. "No, I can't. I can't."

She turned on her heel and walked away from the Hall of Ferocious Jade, even as the examiner behind her swore, even as the door closed and locked with the thud of an executioner's blade. It separated her from the life that she had planned on living, and she realized, as she broke into a run, that she didn't care about it at all, not really.

She ran all the way down to the docks, where a crew of sailors were trying to find a way to load the snarling tiger onto a ship. The poppy had worn off, and the tiger lashed out with tooth and claw at everyone who came near.

"I can help!" Dieu cried. "I can solve this for you!"

The captain looked at her dubiously, taking in her curved shoulders and her meager frame.

"You'd barely be a meal for it," he started.

"No," she insisted. "Listen. I can charm tigers, listen, only listen."

The sailors stopped, because they had no wish to chance the tiger's teeth or claws again, and they stepped back slightly.

"Listen," said Dieu more softly, and she locked eyes with the tiger, always a dangerous thing to do. "Only listen. *My love has gone from me, and I will never again laugh. My love has gone from me and she has taken all light with her.*"

The tiger was silent, glaring from the cage, and the sailors looked skeptical.

"I sit in the moon-viewing pavilion, the hem of my sleeves wet from tears, and I cannot see for the grief has stolen my eyes, and I cannot speak for the grief has stolen my tongue."

The tiger growled, a deep and resonant sound, and Dieu went closer. She was aware of the sailors on the dock, of the clangor of the city behind her, but nothing mattered more than the caged beast in front of her.

"I sit, weeping, eyeless, tongueless, without laughter and absent from light. I sit, and I wait for the answer that only my wife could give."

Finally, the tiger spoke, and her words were soft as a summer wind, as gentle and smooth as Dieu's own.

"I am yours, and so I will be your light and your laughter. I am yours, so open your eyes to look at me, and open your mouth so that I may kiss it. I am yours, I am yours, and nevermore will I leave."

The dock fell silent at the poet's words in the tiger's mouth, and then Dieu opened the cage.

She released the tiger, who with her first bound came out of the cage, and with her second bound, she had swept Scholar Dieu on her back, and with her third bound, she and the scholar were away, and no one ever saw them again.

So, then, is the story of Scholar Dieu and how she wed

the tiger Ho Thi Thao, and how—

~

"No. That's *enough*," said Sinh Loan sharply. "I hate this story, and if you finish it, I shall hate you too."

"I would not want that," Chih said without thinking, and at Sinh Loan's hard look, they coughed a little. "It is only the story as it was told and written and then told to me."

Sinh Cam shook her head.

"I don't think I like it at all," she said finally, "I like the poetry, but . . . But I do not think that's what happened. I don't like Ho Thi Thao in the cage. I don't like that she was waiting for Scholar Dieu to free her because she couldn't do it herself. I don't *like* it."

"Because it isn't true," snapped Sinh Loan. "It's something stupid that humans made up. Imagine thinking that a little scholar could tame a tiger with poetry and a few nights of love, what foolishness."

"Madam . . ." Chih began, and for just a moment, a certain tension in Sinh Loan's shoulders, a certain single-minded set to her grass-green eyes suggested that the tiger had decided to end the storytelling once and for all.

Then Si-yu spoke up, her voice calm as if she couldn't see the tiger's killing look or the way that Piluk was snorting, throwing her trunk from side to side and shuffling her broad feet.

"Well, then? What's the real story?"

Sinh Loan glared at her and nodded angrily.

"Fine. If only so you do not die believing that terrible nonsense."

~

Ho Thi Thao stalked the streets of Ahnfi for three days and three nights, and by the end of that time, every door was barred against her, and her sides were as hollow as a drum. She killed, for she was angry, and she did not eat what she killed, for she was heartsick.

Instead she grew slower and more tired, and her head swam with taunting ghosts and bright lights. A tiger cannot go so very long without eating, and Ho Thi Thao's days of young starvation were long behind her. She ached with hunger, and the fire that lived in her heart was apt to go out.

Finally, late one night, she found Dieu, who had married again, dressed in red robes edged with black, her face as pale as moonlight on snow. She smelled of unhappiness, and she smelled of regret, and she stood in a golden cage that kept her back from the tumult of the city.

"Well, haven't you done well for yourself," Ho Thi

Thao said angrily. "Look at how many people have come to your wedding, and how very happy you are!"

"I am not happy at all," Dieu said, her face full of sorrow. "I have made a terrible mistake."

"And what mistake was that?" asked Ho Thi Thao, who wanted to hear every evil thing she could about Dieu's new spouse.

"I have wronged you," Dieu said to Ho Thi Thao's surprise. "I was wrong to leave you. I was wrong to starve you. If you let me feed you now, I will go home with you to the mountains, and yours will be the only name I speak at night."

"I don't even know your name," said Ho Thi Thao haughtily. "I have not asked for it."

"Ask me for it now," Dieu begged, but Ho Thi Thao, even starving, was possessed of a terrible pride.

"I will not ask for the name of a woman wearing her bridal clothes," Ho Thi Thao said with dignity.

"Fine," said Dieu, and in the golden cage with all the wedding guests watching in horror and fascination, she stripped off her robes. First came the fine red clothes trimmed in black, and then came the pale green underrobe that was sheer enough that it could be shredded with a breath. Then there was her skirt, which she kicked off, and then the embroidered band that fit over her breasts.

"I am keeping the shoes on," Dieu said.

"I don't care about that at all," said Ho Thi Thao, looking her up and down.

"Ask me for my name now."

"I am too hungry to think of that," said Ho Thi Thao, even as she could feel the ground slipping underneath her feet. "I will not eat unless it is from your hands."

Dieu did not hesitate. She brought her hand up to her mouth, and though her teeth were small and sad human things, she snapped them together on the heel of her hand until the blood ran and Ho Thi Thao grew faint from hunger and from love.

Dieu reached her red hand between the bars of her cage, and greedily, Ho Thi Thao lapped up her blood, taking Dieu's hand in her mouth for a single moment before she remembered herself. When she let go, she was dizzy with bliss, and when she turned back to Dieu, there was a happy smile on her face.

"Ask me for my name," Dieu said, and Ho Thi Thao nodded obediently.

"Give me your name," she said. "I want it now."

"My name is Trung Dieu," she said, and with a single blow, the tiger broke the bars on her cage and carried her away amidst the shouting of her would-be husband and his family.

Together, they ran all the way back to the Boarback

Mountains, and for the rest of their nights together, Ho Thi Thao would eat every meal from her wife's fingers and kiss the scar on her hand before she went on to kiss the rest of her as well. They lived well-fed until they were only bones, and even their bones were happy, turning white and sharp as teeth in the moonlight.

Chapter Eleven

ALL SIX OF THEM, seven if you counted Piluk, were silent as Sinh Loan ended her story. Chih wondered if the sky behind the tigers was growing a little lighter, if the air was a little warmer and easier to breathe.

"Thank you very much for your story, madam," Chih said, stretching out their writing hand. "I am very grateful that you decided to tell it to us."

"You should be," Sinh Loan said shortly, "and I hope you took very good notes, because now we are going to eat you."

"Oh don't," exclaimed Sinh Cam, and her elder sister turned to her in annoyance.

"I am hungry, and I am sure that you are as well . . ."

"I'll go down and get us a cow from the lowland farms," said Sinh Cam, "or I can bring us back a farmer if I cannot find a cow. Only I want to hear the cleric tell us another story."

"They're not going to be any better," argued Sinh Loan.

"Then we can fix them," replied Sinh Cam earnestly,

but Sinh Loan shook her head.

"I'm tired of fixing things," she said. "I am bored, and I am stiff, and I am hungry, and if you had a grain of common sense, you would be too . . ."

Their raised voices woke Sinh Hoa, who reached out to cuff blindly at whichever of her sisters she could reach. It was Sinh Loan instead of Sinh Cam, unfortunately, which got her a sharp smack to the nose, which made her grunt and wake up a little more.

Si-yu leaned in closer to Chih, grabbing their arm.

"All right, when I give you the signal, run under Piluk's legs."

Chih didn't have enough time to ask what the signal was when Si-yu uttered a piercing whistle, two high notes with the final one swooping low.

Piluk grunted loudly in response and took three steps backwards, putting her broad rear to the corner of the barn and lowering her head so that her short horns were positioned to gore.

Oh, that must have been the signal, Chih thought, already moving, and they dashed blindly towards the mammoth's legs. Si-yu was right behind her, and when Chih slid to their knees, half-blinded by Piluk's hanging fur, they turned just in time to see Bao-so getting shoved towards them.

"Pull him in, pull him in!" Si-yu was shouting, and Chih

gritted their teeth and, latching their hands onto Bao-so's coat, dragged him back as far as they could. They were blinded by fur, they were sweating under their coat, and they were in terror of Piluk's feet, stomping up and down.

They drill so that their feet come up and down in the same place, Chih thought desperately, but they wrapped their arms around Bao-so, grabbing on to his body as tightly as they could and keeping him close to the space directly under Piluk's belly.

"Come on then!" Si-yu shouted. Her voice came from above, and Chih realized that she had scrambled up into her saddle again. There were two loud thumping sounds, Si-yu's lance against the rafters. "I'm tired of you talking about eating us, come and eat us if you think you can."

"Actually, please don't," Chih muttered, too numb and tired to be anything more emphatic than that.

Through the space between Piluk's forelegs, Chih saw three tigers and not two and a woman any longer. They looked as enormous as cart horses, and even if the two smaller ones hung back, the third was large enough and hungry enough to make up for it.

"*Think* I can, little scout? I do more than think it. What do *you* think you are doing, with that little stick and your squealing calf? I told you I would let her go if I ate you, but if she is hurt protecting you, I won't care."

One of the younger sisters, Sinh Hoa, Chih thought,

made a sudden dash forward, cutting left so fast that Chih only caught a glimpse of green eyes and a velvet muzzle wrinkled in ferocity. Her hunting roar turned into a shriek as Piluk swung trunk and tusk hard at Si-yu's call, and then a hefty thwack against the tiger's hindquarters sent her scampering back for cover.

Sinh Hoa hung back, but Sinh Loan came forward, head lowered and her paws barely clearing the ground.

"How long do you think you can last?" she asked, as if she were terribly interested in the answer. "One mammoth, one lance, one half-dead man and one weaponless cleric with bad stories . . ."

To Chih's surprise, Si-yu laughed, the sound bright and wild.

"Oh, I should say for just a brief count longer, madam," she said. "Just another little while . . ."

Then it came, a low and throbbing roar that seemed to hit the lightening sky and bounce back, a sound that up close would be a wall and from far away still had a weight that could crush. Piluk squeaked, stamping her forefeet up and down as Chih yelped with panic, and then she bugled in return, her voice higher and less powerful than the first call, but just as carrying.

Chih would have cheered, but then Si-yu shrieked and Piluk screamed, rearing up in panic as a furry orange and black shape rolled off her back to thump to the ground below, followed immediately after by Si-yu, lance falling from her hand.

It was Sinh Cam, Chih realized, who must have scaled the bales of hay by the wall to jump down from the rafters. Sinh Cam shook off her stunning and put her teeth into Si-yu's back as Chih stared in silent panic. Before they could break it however, Piluk lunged forward, but now the other two tigers swarmed her. Chih flattened herself on the ground just in time to avoid a stunning blow from one of Piluk's rear legs, and they looked up to see Piluk toss her large head and throw Sinh Cam off of Si-yu's body.

Sinh Loan, obvious in her larger size, roared, and she threw herself up towards Piluk's saddle. If she could get a good grip, if she could reach the back of Piluk's neck . . .

Then there was a deep bass thundering, and two more mammoths, one the classic russet red, the other with patches of gray over her eyes, rammed into the space, filling it as much with their trumpeting as they did with their bulk. With a curse, Chih dragged Bao-so's prone form back to the corner, because trampling was as nasty a fate as being eaten. They had just turned around when there was a final scream from the tigers and everything went still.

I'm still alive, Chih thought with surprise. *Or I will be as long as my heart doesn't beat out of my chest . . .*

"Anyone alive down there? I see . . . that's Piluk, isn't it? Si-yu, Si-yu, girl, where are you?"

There was a long moment in the fallen hay bales and the forest of treelike legs when Chih was afraid there would be no answer.

"Here! Over here, damnit, Hyun-lee, move Malli back before she scares Piluk even more."

Upon hearing Si-yu's indignant voice, Chih collapsed back against the back of the barn, letting themselves shake to little bits as they had wanted to do since all of this started. They felt as if they were swimming in sweat, and all of the strength that they had been using to sit up straight and talk to tigers abruptly deserted them.

When they looked up next, there was an intent-looking man working over Bao-so, and a tall fat woman was offering them a hand up. Chih took it without thinking and then nearly stumbled into the woman's arms before she set them upright again. Si-yu clapped them on the shoulder with a grin.

"Didn't think we'd make it out of *that*, did you?" she asked.

Before Chih could respond, the man who had been tending Bao-so hauled him up to his feet, one shoulder shoved under his armpit to support him. To Chih's surprise, Bao-so was awake, and though his eyes were a little vague, they could see the sense in them.

"We should bring out a medic to look him over and a holy man to make sure that nothing came to live in him while he was down."

The tall woman nodded, and Chih, despite their exhaustion, noted with interest that the coil of mammoth hair pinned at her shoulder was beaded with carved ivory beads where Si-yu's was bare.

"Good thing for you we were escorting the Great Star himself up through to Borsoon. We would have camped at sundown, but Malli was all twitchy, wouldn't stop, and you know if Malli won't, then Sooni won't, either."

Si-yu looked up from comforting Piluk with a grin.

"Lucky for all of us. Thanks for the rescue. I was afraid the cleric was going to run out of story before you got here, but it turns out there was just enough."

"How in the world did you know that they were coming?" asked Chih, and Si-yu laughed.

"I didn't. Piluk did. She started to get excited a little while ago. She was talking to someone, and she's no dummy, my baby, is she?" cooed Si-yu, leaning up to thump Piluk's shoulder. The mammoth swayed in a way that was decidedly smug, and her trunk knocked against her rider's hip with pleasure.

"How did she know?" asked Chih, baffled.

"Calls we can't hear," said Hyun-lee. "That's what I think it is, anyway."

"Uncle says it's a kinship connection, that they can always talk to their relatives no matter how far apart they are. Piluk is Malli's third cousin on her dam's side. That would do it."

"Your uncle still thinks that they should get meat every solstice. That's not right."

Abruptly, they both seemed to remember that Chih was there. They couldn't quite tell if the pair were embarrassed to be caught quibbling or protecting trade secrets, but Hyun-lee changed the topic abruptly.

"And you, cleric. What's your story?"

"I needed to get through the pass and then south to Kephi. Si-yu was kind enough to escort me up to the way station, and then . . . tigers."

Hyun-lee laughed, her eyes lost in the cheerful lines of her face.

"*And then tigers* sounds about right. Those are probably the three they were talking about on the circuit. We'll keep an eye out. Ingrusk will probably set a bounty on their hides before too long."

Chih couldn't help feel a pang of regret at the fact. It wasn't as if bounties weren't set on human outlaws as well as tigers, but it seemed . . . a shame, perhaps. If they hung Sinh Loan's skull on the ice wall at Ingrusk, the only place she would live on was in the archives of Singing Hills.

"Well, Borsoon's a little out of your way, but you can

likely hitch a ride from there," said Hyun-lee, coming to a decision.

"But . . . we're going to sleep first, right?" asked Chih plaintively, and Hyun-lee slapped them jovially on the shoulder.

"Of course, we're not savages. Go ahead and go lie down in the way station. You look like something the mammoth trampled flat."

Chih turned straight into a hug from Si-yu.

"You did pretty good for an out-of-shape southerner," she said cheerfully. "Get some sleep. Dream of meat."

Chih was so shaky on their legs that they thought they might collapse before they got to the door of the way station. The ground seemed to tilt underneath them, and they kept seeing flashes of orange and black out of the corner of their eyes.

They were close to falling asleep on their feet, but then something made them turn their head, and they stared.

The big bull stalked the edge of the clearing, ears standing out from his head, and tossing his head from side to side. He wasn't saddled, but his curving tusks were capped with polished steel, and they guessed that his back was easily level with the roof of the way station, far larger than the cows, far heavier and mountainous.

Royal mammoth, Chih's mind supplied. *They crossed the Ko-anam Fords. One just like this broke the gates of the*

Palace of Gleaming Light, letting the winter into Anh . . .

Chih froze as the one that Hyun-lee had called the Great Star—*he must be going to stud at the stables in Borsoon, I wonder if they would let me go see*—stamped one last time at the edge of the clearing, snorted, and then wandered up to Chih. They stood stock still as the royal mammoth leaned down and his trunk came up to knock back their hood and sniff curiously at Chih's head. The bull's touch was surprisingly delicate and now Chih could see the phlanges, one above and one below the flaring nostrils, mobile enough to wrap around branches and grab and pinch. Up close, the bull was overwhelming, a wall of solid muscle and fur that could trample an empire flat.

"Hello," Chih said softly. "I wish Almost Brilliant could see you . . ."

The bull abruptly decided that Chih was fine, and turned to patrol the edge of the clearing again, and after one last look to reassure themself that there were no tigers around, Chih went into the way station.

Acknowledgments

First, thank you to Ruoxi Chen, editor extraordinaire, who gets my work like few ever have and who unfailingly cheers me on, and to my agent, Diana Fox, who has always encouraged me to be my best and least restrained self.

The team at Tordotcom Publishing has been amazing—so much love to Lauren Hougen, Mordicai Knode, Caroline Perny, Amanda Melfi, Sanaa Ali-Virani, Christine Foltzer, Lauren Anesta, and Irene Gallo!

Alyssa Winans, of course, continues to knock it outta the park with this cover, and I couldn't stop staring or smiling when I saw it for the first time.

Thank you as always to Cris Chingwa, Victoria Coy, Leah Kolman, Amy Lepke, and Meredy Shipp!

And of course, once again, thank you to Shane Hochstetler, Grace Palmer, and Carolyn Mulroney. I couldn't ask for a better set of humans to call my own.

Life's weird and only getting weirder by the day. I'm so grateful that I have the right people to share it with.

About the Author

NGHI VO was born in central Illinois, and she retains a healthy respect of and love for corn mazes, scarecrows, and fifty-year floods. These days, she lives on the shores of Lake Michigan, which is less a lake than an inland sea that she is sure is just biding its time.

Her short fiction has appeared in *Strange Horizons, Uncanny Magazine, PodCastle, Lightspeed,* and *Fireside.* Her short story "Neither Witch nor Fairy" made the 2014 Otherwise Award Honor List. Nghi mostly writes about food, death, and family, but sometimes detours into blood, love, and rhetoric. She believes in the ritual of lipstick, the power of stories, and the right to change your mind.

TOR·COM

Science fiction. Fantasy. The universe.

And related subjects.

*

More than just a publisher's website, *Tor.com* is a venue for **original fiction, comics,** and **discussion** of the entire field of SF and fantasy, in all media and from all sources. Visit our site today—and join the conversation yourself.